Visible and Invisible

FAITH AND SHADOWS
BOOK ONE

JENNI DEWITT

Editing by EJL Editing | www.ejlediting.com/

Cover Design by Moonpress | www.moonpress.co

First edition 2023

www.jennidewitt.com

For Justin, Tony, and Cooper

Chapter One

Sleep beckoned to Eva like delicate tendrils of smoke. She tumbled backward into exhaustion, giving into its temptation. Fear stabbed her as she saw people running over the hill toward her with terrified expressions and flailing arms. Something was wrong. She moved toward the center of the house, calling to her friends to take cover. She crouched down and waited, but no one responded. They were running out of time!

She sprinted from the bedroom to the living room, whipping her head around as she searched for her friends. The large windows were a magnet pulling her gaze. A huge, horrible mountain of water was rushing toward the house. The people outside were running in a hopeless attempt to escape it.

As the water barreled down on the house, Eva threw her arms over her head and braced for the impact. When it hit, the windows would shatter. The roof would splinter.

Seconds ticked by and nothing happened. She peeked out from under her arms. The wave had passed. In its wake, a trail of bodies lay on the soggy ground. The few people who survived were running toward her house, which remained untouched.

Eva sprinted to the door and flung it open to let the people inside. She saw the reason they were still running. Three horrible, pure black tornados devoid of any light twisted and turned in a path straight toward them.

Eva screamed, or at least she tried to. Leaving the door open, she tripped over furniture, banging her knees as she shouted for her friends again. Where were they?

She spotted them in Jai'Lune's car outside. They were laughing and smiling as if they were clueless to what was going on around them. Eva bolted out the door and ran toward them. "We have to get inside! The tornados are coming!" They gave her blank stares. Her long, brown hair whipped in the violent wind, creating a storm of its own as she ran closer, fighting the wind to get to them.

Eva woke up, gasping for air. Her gray t-shirt clung to her back, drenched in sweat. She shoved the damp tendrils of hair away from her face and peered around, frustration pulling at the corners of her consciousness and hands trembling. She resisted the urge to nibble her one remaining long fingernail.

Her battered math notebook caught her attention where it teetered on the edge of her bed. She scooped it up and squinted through tired eyes at the sloppy handwriting. The last problem was half done. Great, now she was falling asleep mid math problem. She tossed her homework on the floor with a thud. No way she was finishing it tonight; she'd have to do it in the morning.

Eva pulled her purple quilt—a relic from her fifth birthday—up to her chin the way she had when she was little. When Gram gave the quilt to her, she said, "I made it with love." In her little kid mind, she had imagined Gram's love was literally woven into the blanket. She used to wrap it around her and pretend it was Gram giving her a hug every night when she went to bed.

A movement on Eva's left distracted her from the memory. She turned to see her dog, Flip, resting his head on the edge of the bed. Flip's gaze seemed to ask, *You okay*? His shiny brown eyes were genuine, but his hair stuck up in such a ridiculous way she couldn't help but smile. She stuck her hand out of the covers to rub his soft fur.

Outside, she could hear the wind rushing over the Nebraska plains as it hit the outside of her small, yellow house. It blew past, reminding her of the group of people in her dream, off to places unknown. The tornados still haunted Eva, but she needed to get some sleep.

Eva forced herself to focus on the trees outside her window, standing solid and reliable in her front yard. Pretty soon they'd burst into red flames, leaves glowing bright as a Nebraska sunset. In her town, too small to be a map dot, the trees were a local attraction. People would ride by on their bikes and stop to take pictures.

She imagined her tire swing hanging from a long rope in the tree where her grandpa tied it as a surprise for her tenth birthday. Eva pictured it blowing in the wind as if carrying an invisible passenger. Her eyelids were heavy.

Then she was running through a cornfield. The sharp leaves on the cornstalks cut at her bare legs. Her breath came fast as she tried to keep up with the people running beside her. Eva glanced over and saw Grace O'Donnell, her classmate since kindergarten, red hair streaming behind her like a warning flag and bright blue eyes flashing with fear.

To Eva's left, her classmate Alex was running beside her. Even amid his terror, he ran with the grace of an athlete. His biceps strained against his t-shirt as he pumped his arms.

Eva dared a glance over her shoulder, trying to figure out why they were running. Three pure black tornados ripped toward them as if they might cut the night sky open and pour out their unspeakable darkness. Her heart pounded in her chest as she willed her clumsy legs to move faster.

After an eternity, they reached the edge of town and ran to the closest building—the church. Alex jerked on the ancient wood door, and it sprang open. They all shoved inside, and the slamming door blocked her view of the tornados.

They turned in unison and Eva saw familiar faces staring back at her from the pews as time stood still for two clicks of the clock. Then Grace shouted, "They're coming! The tornados are coming! We have to take shelter!"

Eva, Alex, and Grace bolted for cover, but the people in the pews sat staring, their confusion morphing into annoyance. Then they turned their backs, dismissing Eva's group without words. She bolted from her hiding spot and ran to the front of the church, desperate to get their attention.

The pastor strode toward her as if he intended to stop this nonsense, long white robes billowing behind him. Eva ran in the opposite direction, searching for shelter. Country music blared over the church speakers and Eva opened her eyes. After a moment of confusion, she realized she was in her own bedroom. Not a church.

Eva pushed the snooze button on her phone alarm to silence the music and laid back, a sense of dread rising in her like a bottle filling with water. Two nightmares in one night. That was a first. It was getting worse. Much worse.

The weight of the dreams pinned Eva to her bed, but she needed to get up for school. She sucked in extra air and let it out in a rush, trying to calm herself. She had to get it together.

Mom might be home from work. Hopefully, she wasn't in one of her bad moods again. Eva remembered the days when her mom used to stroke her hair and tell her everything would be okay. Those days were gone. No more comforting ice cream for breakfast unless she got it herself.

Eva shook her head. She didn't need anyone to get her ice cream. She was seventeen and perfectly capable of taking care of herself. She got out of bed with one eye squinting and the other closed. She didn't need the lights on. After a decade in the same house, she had every nook and cranny memorized.

Eva wiggled into her favorite faded jeans and pulled on a teal shirt that matched the color of her eyes. She splashed cold water on her face and dabbed it with a towel, then grabbed her mom's mascara and made a few quick strokes. Finally, she was returning to the land of the living.

As she walked to school, Eva stole a few extra minutes to read. She lifted her feet out of habit at the spots in the sidewalk where the tree roots had shoved the cement up into tiny mountain ranges. As she got to the school, Jai'Lune fell in beside her. Eva snapped her book shut and shoved it into her book bag.

"How about that horrible math assignment? Did you figure it out?" Jai'Lune asked.

"Barely. It's a great way to fight insomnia, though."

"True!" Jai'Lune's laugh was a melody floating in the air.

"What are you wearing?" Eva was no fashion queen, but even she couldn't miss Jai'Lune's overalls, straw hat, and pink cowboy boots.

"It's spirit week! My ancestors were a bunch of hicks, and I'm representing that fine lineage. I was going to chew on some straw for effect, but I kept sneezing."

Eva groaned and smacked her head. They were supposed to dress up as their ancestors. She didn't give two hoots about some stupid spirit week, but Jai'Lune always got into it. She had a pang of guilt. *Maybe she should try harder.*

Then again, her ancestors were a bunch of cow-milking,

squirrel-eating farmers who spent their life trying not to freeze to death in the cold Nebraska winters. A life of survival. Eva glanced down at her clothes and shrugged. Good enough. After all, wasn't she trying to survive her last year of high school?

When they reached the old brick school, Eva pulled the heavy front door open. They stepped inside as Grace strode by in traditional Irish dress. The memory of her dream slammed into Eva, catching her off guard. She took a deep breath. *Get it together, Eva.*

The day was a tired monster slogging by. As Eva waited in line for her tray of meatloaf-surprise, she scanned the room for a place to sit where she could blend in without being too awkward. Nothing had changed in the lunchroom for decades —not even the lunch lady. The tables had wheels and folded in half. Their light-brown tops were tired and worn from generations of lunch trays and soapy rags.

Finally, Eva made it to the front of the line. The lunch lady greeted her with the same scowl she probably gave Eva's mom twenty years ago. *Maybe she's some sort of eternal mutant alien. Mutant Lunch Lady—that could be a good book.*

Eva sat at the end of the speech team table and heard them talking about Alex and Janet. They'd broken up... again. *Surprise, surprise.* The story got less and less interesting every time. Janet got jealous of Alex. Alex got annoyed with her. It was mind-numbing. *Since no one ends up with their high school sweetheart anyhow, what's the point?*

Eva let her hair fall forward, blocking out the world as her mind drifted. The dreams were happening every night, a cartoon storm cloud following her around. She was losing hope they would ever stop. Somehow, each night was more terrifying than the one before.

Maybe she should research tornados? If she understood the dreams, they might stop. At least it was something to try. The thought of it made her feel less helpless. The bell blared and Eva jumped, bumping into the girl next to her. "Geez!" the girl shouted.

"Sorry," Eva said as she bolted to go dump her tray. The school was built in 1910 and had about a million floors. She had to climb three of them to get to class on time. As the late bell rang, she slid into the seat Jai'Lune saved for her.

Eva sighed. She might be sweaty from climbing Mount Marysburg High, but she was on time. Alex slid into the seat next to her with a smirk. There were no assigned seats, but everyone sat in the same spot every day. Everyone except Alex. Each day, he sat in a new spot like he was desperate to keep life interesting.

The way people reacted always made Eva smile. They'd come in and see their normal spot taken. They'd spin in a complete circle and end up sitting in the broken desk in the back, even though there were plenty of other options.

The teacher interrupted Eva's thoughts. "Open your books. You're going to do your assignment with a partner today. Let's count off." Eva stifled a groan, wondering who she'd get stuck with this time.

Mrs. Buckle moved around the classroom, her arm serving as the Grim Reaper while she dictated the pairs. When Eva realized Grace was her partner, she relaxed a little. It could have been worse. Grace was a cheerleader, but she'd always been nice to Eva. She remembered Grace walking up to the school every day with a drove of brothers and sisters trailing behind her. It always made Eva wonder how it would feel to have siblings. She'd probably never know.

"Hey, Eva!" Grace said, flashing her pretty smile as she sat down.

"Hi," Eva said, her voice coming out as a squeak.

"Do you understand this?" Grace asked. "It's insanely confusing!"

"Yeah, it's hard, but I think I'm getting it."

It surprised Eva what a good team she and Grace made. When one of them didn't understand a problem, the other did. "Ten minutes left," Mrs. Buckle announced. "Ask questions if you have them."

The football players at the next table smirked at Grace. "Hey, Grace, I got a question. Whatcha doing Friday night?"

Grace rolled her eyes and turned her back on them. Eva smiled. No one ignored the football players. They were gods in their small town. You'd think they went off to war, not some stupid football game every Friday night, the way everyone worshipped them.

They weren't gods, though. Eva shivered, remembering eighth grade when they spent the entire year barking at her every time they walked past. They'd found her mom's senior picture in one of those giant, dusty pages of class pictures hanging in the hall. "Your mom was a smokin' hot babe. What's wrong with you? Your dad must have been a dog." She'd faked more stomachaches that year than she had her whole life.

Eva realized she was spacing off and snuck a glance at Grace. She knew she should offer some polite chitchat. It was the Nebraska way. Why couldn't she ever think of anything normal to say? *Come on Eva, it's not that hard. People do it all the time.*

She was grateful when Grace filled the silence between them. "Have anything fun planned for the weekend?"

"Nope. How about you?" People loved talking about themselves. She figured out a few years ago if you could get them talking about themselves, it was easier to keep the conversation going.

"I think I might go to the lake with some people tomorrow. It's supposed to get arctic next week. This might be our last chance."

"That sounds fun," Eva said, trying to sound convincing. A part of her wondered what it was like to be popular, go to cool parties and hang out with guys. But it was such a tiny part of her. The bell rang, and the class bolted out of their seats, headed for their next destination.

When the last bell rang, Eva shoved her way through the crowded hall to her locker, grabbed her heavy bookbag, and raced out of school like a prisoner on jailbreak. She was trying not to be late again for her shift at the nursing home.

As she walked, the gentle breeze brushed Eva's face and carried with it the smell of change. She held her arms out at her sides as she walked through the falling leaves. She loved fall —nature's dramatic flair before it gave up the ghost and succumbed to winter.

A leaf began its final descent in front of her and she paused, tilting her face upward to enjoy the show. She had the sense she was being watched and turned to see Alex, football helmet in hand, staring at her from half a block away. Eva blushed and spun around, hurrying her steps toward home.

Chapter Two

Alex had never paid much attention to Eva. Until now. What was it about her? At lunch, she caught his attention and again during math. Maybe she'd walked home right in front of him a thousand times. How did he miss it? He watched her stop to let a leaf fall to the ground in front of her. She was unique compared to the other girls at school. It intrigued him.

Alex shook his head to clear it and headed to practice. When he got to the field, some guys were already jogging laps. He fell in beside them. They talked and joked with each other, but he stayed quiet. From experience, he knew that whenever he tried to join the banter, it turned out awkward.

Maybe he shouldn't be surprised. They had nothing in common. His teammates watched mindless videos, and he was a book nerd. They loved to fix up cars, and he preferred to go fishing. For years, he'd tried to fit in and care about the stuff they were interested in because he wanted a friend. Any friend. Please God. But it was exhausting to pretend to be someone he wasn't.

At Marysburg High, Alex was a square peg trying to fit

into a round hole. He was too nerdy for the jocks and too much of a jock to fit in with the nerds. Still, there had to be someone out there like him, didn't there? Maybe next year at college he'd find his people. Mom kept saying he would. Alex wanted to believe her.

At least when he dated Janet, he wasn't as lonely. She always made plans for them, and they hung out with her friends. It made life easier and, if he was being honest with himself, it was part of the reason he stayed with her longer than he should have. He didn't want to be lonely. But he wouldn't give into his loneliness, or her tricks to win him back, this time. That was over.

They finished warm-ups and practice went into full swing. Alex welcomed the physical exhaustion. It quieted his mind and gave him an escape from his thoughts and this tiny town. After practice, he grabbed his bag from the locker room and headed out. His familiar, old rusty pickup made him smile. He'd never forget the day Pops handed him the keys on his sixteenth birthday. The truck was his ticket to freedom.

He couldn't have saved up enough money for it on his own. Thanks to all the extra sports camps and practices, he couldn't hold down a decent job. He didn't want to be indebted to his dad, either. He hated the way his dad held it over his head with all the if you want to live under my roof talk. Pops would never do that to him.

The road home was two miles of highway and two miles of gravel, the perfect time to clear his head. He was enjoying the drive when, out of nowhere, something was closing around his neck. His truck slid right and left as he tried to claw away whatever was squeezing his throat, but he couldn't get a hold of anything. He managed to guide his truck to the side of the road and slammed on the brakes, throwing it into park.

Pawing at his neck, he connected with something scaly and warm. He grabbed it and pulled with all his might. The pressure loosened for a fraction of a second and he gasped for precious air, glancing down at what he held in his hands. Nothing. He was clutching something solid. He could feel it, but nothing was there. How could he defend himself from something he couldn't see?

The pressure around his neck tightened again. Alex acted on instinct, punching the air in front of him and swinging his elbows. The pressure released suddenly, and he hopped out of his pickup. It was gone, whatever it was. As fast as it began, the bizarre encounter was over.

To calm himself, Alex took deep breaths of the fresh country air. He walked around his pickup and stood peering out at the field. *What was that?*

Dread crept through his veins as it did when he woke from the dreams. Alex shook his head, trying to shake off the feeling the way he did after a tackle, but physical pain was easier to escape than emotional pain.

Without thinking, Alex hopped the barbed-wire fence and was in the field in a few strides. The alfalfa came up to his knees. Pops would cut it and let it dry on the ground soon, then bale it for the cattle to eat that winter. But right now, it was alive with purple flowers blooming on the tips of each delicate green branch. He dodged the plants as best he could, a pang of guilt hitting him every time he heard a snap of the delicate branches.

When he reached the creek, Alex knelt in the mud and splashed the stream's cold water on his face. It brought him back to reality a bit, and he stood up, realizing he was in a field wearing nothing but cowboy boots and athletic shorts. Good thing nature was a judgment-free zone. It didn't care that he'd worn his cowboy boots to school that day and didn't have any other shoes when he took off his cleats. It was oblivious to the fact that he drove home shirtless this time of year to cool down after practice. Out here, he could simply be himself.

Alex plopped down on a rock on the bank. His mind was fighting to find calm, and the sound of water trickling over rocks quieted his thoughts. Maybe he should tell Pops about the dreams. He'd know what to do. Pops always knew what to do. The idea comforted Alex, and he stood up to head back to the pickup.

~

At supper, Alex's dad asked how practice was. Alex walked him through everything they did. Dad nodded in approval. "You think the team's ready?" he asked. Their first game of the season was that week.

"I think so. The other team lost a lot of seniors. Should be able to catch a win." *I hope.* Dad was always crabby for a week if they lost.

His dad smiled. "Should be a good game. Make sure you're keeping your shoulder down. We don't need you getting injured right before the recruiters come around."

"Yes sir," Alex responded, out of duty or habit. He wasn't sure which.

He thought of the letters Dad had neatly stacked in a row on the old desk in their home office. When Alex was a freshman, they'd come from no-name colleges interested in what he could do. But as a sophomore and junior, the names on the letters were from slightly bigger colleges, ones he'd at least heard of before. Dad was hoping for the big names this year. Alex wasn't even sure he wanted to play football in college, but there was no saying that to his dad. Alex didn't have the heart to take that dream away from him.

Truth be told, Alex was still trying to figure out what *he* wanted to do. Leave this town. That's the one thing he knew for sure. He'd come back to see Pops and his mom. Maybe not every weekend, but more often than his brother did. The pang of missing his brother hit his heart in that old, familiar way. Alex tried to ignore it. Trent graduated five years ago. Dad had been even harder on him than he was on Alex. Once Trent got out, he never looked back. Alex wasn't sure he could blame him. Still, the hole his absence left stung. Not that they were even that close.

Alex had always been the annoying little brother to Trent. He tried everything to make Trent think he was cool, bringing him snacks when he played video games and doing his chores. He even joined the football team as a manager to get more time with his brother. But no matter how much he tried, he was always invisible to his brother. *The same way he was to everyone else.*

"Honey?" Alex's mom said, snapping him out of his thoughts.

"Yeah?"

"Everything okay? You've been kind of... out of it lately," she said.

"You're not moping around about that girl again, are you? What's her name? Jenni, Jane. You better not let that mess with your game," his dad huffed.

"It's Janet. Her name is Janet. For goodness sakes, Travis, they dated for three years," Alex's mom said.

"Well, I can't keep up with all their teenage drama. I have enough of my own problems to worry about."

His mom pushed her lips together and rolled her eyes. But she'd learned long ago, as they all had, to keep her mouth shut. Otherwise, he'd go on another rant and sometimes even leave for days, and they wouldn't know when he was coming back. She turned her attention back to Alex. "What were your highs and lows today, honey?"

Mom had learned this so-called game when she was co-teaching the Wednesday night CCD classes at their church. You were supposed to think of the best and worst part of your day and spill the beans about it. She'd take mental notes and bring it back to her prayer group to pray over. As if Alex needed his business spread around town by those gossipy church ladies. He made sure to keep it all surface level. "High—practice was good. Low—I have math homework."

It was obvious she was hoping for more, and the guilt tried to sneak up on Alex again, but he shoved it back down. It was the best he could give her right now. She patted his arm. "Okay, honey, that's nice."

Maybe—somehow—she knew.

Chapter Three

After school, Eva stepped through her unlocked front door. They'd lost the key years ago and never got a new one. What was the point? Old Mrs. Cotner, the snoopy lady next door, was twice as good as any lock or security system. Gramps always said secrets could hide in a small town. As far as she could tell, no secrets could survive here.

She rode her bike to work so she could enjoy her last few moments of the beautiful day. When she got off work, it would be dark. As she rode, the mums caught her eye as they burst out of flower boxes in enormous circles of bright orange and deep pink. The pool was sad and lonely waiting for winter. Eva clocked in at exactly 3:47, only two minutes late. The head cook, Roxie, gave her the usual welcoming glare. Eva returned her glare with a shrug and got to work. What was it with crabby, old lunch ladies? *Mutant Lunch Lady strikes again.*

Eva loved her job because of the residents. Their stories were amazing. One old guy told her about being a paperboy in Chicago during World War II. Another guy told her stories about living in Wyoming when it was still the Wild West. He had to take his pistol with him to deposit the money from his bar in the bank every night. A conversation with the residents was a stroll through history. Their parents drove horses and now cars can drive themselves. It was amazing.

Jai'Lune worked at the Care Center, too, but she was a nurse's aide. You couldn't pay Eva enough to do that job. She preferred to stay as far away from bathroom duty as possible. Her job was easy. Set the tables, serve the food, clean up afterward, repeat. She finished loading her trusty plastic cart and headed out to set tables.

A few minutes later, people filled the dining room, and it was time to serve supper. She was carrying a plate to the table where the Alzheimer's patients sat and one of them reached out with shocking speed and grabbed her arm. The woman stared at Eva and said, "The dreams mean something. You need to figure out how to stop them."

"Huh?" Eva said, pulling her arm away fast. "What, what do you mean?" But the haze of Alzheimer's had already settled back into the old woman's eyes.

The haunting experience stuck with Eva as she finished her shift. She couldn't shake the momentary clarity and urgency in the old woman's eyes. Could she be talking about the tornado dreams? But how could she possibly know about them? Eva had told no one, not even Jai'Lune, about them yet.

Eva shook her head. The woman couldn't know. It was impossible. An Alzheimer's side effect was all it could be. She put her head down and tried to focus on scraping the uneaten food off the plates.

"Excuse me?" Eva jumped and the plastic plate she was holding clattered to the ground. Her heart slowed a bit when she saw it was Nora, her favorite resident. Nora's hair was disheveled as always, and her crooked skirt was hiked up too high on one side. The familiar smell of Avon perfume drifted Eva's way, and she smiled. "Sorry about that, Nora. What's up?"

Nora was usually all smiles, but today her bushy eyebrows were crowded together in concern. "Have you seen my sister? I can't find her anywhere. I have a picture of her here. Oh dear, where did I put that?"

Nora rustled through her purse and produced an old picture of two young women in their twenties posing in front of a train station. It must have been windy that day. One of them was holding her hat on her head. The other was holding down her knee-length skirt. "That's me there." Nora pointed to the girl holding her hat. "And there's Mabel. Oh, I need to find her. The tornados are coming. Have you seen her?"

Eva froze at the mention of tornados. *Relax Eva.* The picture was windy. Nora probably confused it with a storm. And Eva happened to know her sister had been dead for decades. "I tell you what, Nora. I'll keep my eye out for your sister. Meanwhile, how about I walk you back to your room, where it's safe?"

Nora evaluated Eva's offer. "Well, I guess that would be okay, but if you don't see her after a little while, come get me. We don't have much time."

"Okay, I will." Nora nodded, and Eva took her arm, noticing the solid bone through her thin skin as she led Nora back to her room. She didn't want Nora to keep worrying, so she tried to distract her. "What'd you have for lunch today? Was it any good?"

Nora's eyebrows drew together in concentration. "You know, I don't remember. But I'm sure it was good. The local café has excellent food." Eva resisted the urge to smack her forehead. Nora didn't even know where she was. How would she remember what she ate for lunch?

They inched along at Nora's pace, slow and shuffling, and it took a while to get back to Nora's room, but Eva didn't want to rush her. By the time they made it, Nora forgot she was worried about her sister. Eva helped Nora into bed and pulled the covers up around her, tucking her in the way Eva's mom used to tuck her in when she was little.

As Eva turned to leave, Nora reached one wrinkled hand up out of the blankets and rested it on her arm. "God bless you, child. Will you read to me for a bit? My eyes are shot, but I love to listen."

Nora's room was small, with a single bed, a nightstand, and a couple of chairs. Eva glanced around the room for a book. The only one she saw was an old Bible sitting on Nora's nightstand under the glow of the lamp. Nora must have sensed her hesitation. "The Bible would be fine, dear."

Eva didn't have any experience with the Bible. She sat down in the old wooden rocker across from Nora's bed and held it in her lap, uncertain what to do next.

With a shrug, she placed her thumbs together and opened the book near the beginning. A dried rose petal rested on the page, giving off a nostalgic smell. Eva moved it aside and scanned the words. They were divided into chapters. She picked the first chapter she saw and read:

Chapter 41 Pharaoh's Dream. *After a lapse of two years, Pharaoh had a dream. He was standing by the Nile, when up out of the Nile came seven cows, fine-looking and fat; they grazed in the reed grass. Behind them seven other cows, poor-looking and gaunt, came up out of the Nile; and standing on the bank of the Nile beside the others, the poor-looking, gaunt cows devoured the seven fine-looking, fat cows. Then Pharaoh woke up.*

He fell asleep again and had another dream. He saw seven ears of grain, fat and healthy, growing on a single stalk. Behind them sprouted seven ears of grain, thin and scorched by the east wind; and the thin ears swallowed up the seven fat, healthy ears. Then Pharaoh woke up—it was a dream!

Eva read on about how Pharaoh tried to have all these people interpret his dreams, but no one knew what they meant. *She could relate.* Having strange dreams that didn't make sense could consume you. Pharaoh brought a guy named Joseph out of prison, because everyone said he was great at interpreting dreams. She leaned closer and read on to see what would happen.

Joseph said to Pharaoh: "Pharaoh's dreams have the same meaning. God has made known to Pharaoh what he is about to do. The seven healthy cows are seven years, and the seven healthy ears are seven years—the same in each dream. The seven thin, bad cows that came up after them are seven years, as are the seven thin ears scorched by the east wind; they are seven years of famine. Things are just as I told Pharaoh: God has revealed to Pharaoh what he is about to do. Seven years of great abundance are now coming throughout the land of Egypt; but seven years of famine will rise up after them, when all the abundance will be forgotten in the land of Egypt. When the famine has exhausted the land, no trace of the abundance will be found in the land because of the famine that follows it, for it will be very severe. That Pharaoh had the same dream twice means that the matter has been confirmed by God and that God will soon bring it about."

The story made the hair on the back of Eva's arms stand up. Could her dreams have a similar meaning to Pharaoh's? Last night, for the first time, she'd had the dream twice in one night. A shiver went through her body. Could that mean something was coming soon?

Eva wished she knew a Joseph who could tell her what the dreams meant. Then again, the story said it was God interpreting the dreams. Joseph was simply reporting back what

God said. Maybe she needed someone who could hear God. She rolled her eyes. *As if that existed anymore.*

Nora let out a quiet snore and Eva realized she was sound asleep. She stole a few minutes to re-read the story to herself, then she put the book on Nora's nightstand and went back to work. But she didn't stop thinking about what she read.

The Pharaoh's dreams were different but had the same theme. Seven good and seven bad things. The tornados were the theme of her dreams. They must be the key. She needed to figure out what they meant.

Eva was sweeping the kitchen floors when the lights flickered. She looked up to see Nora standing there, facing away from her. Nora's body was shimmering, and Eva blinked hard, trying to get her eyes to focus. The lights flickered again, and Nora was gone.

Eva went into the dining room, but Nora wasn't there, and she wasn't in the hallway either. Where had she gone? Baffled, she went to the nurses' station. "Hey, Nora's out wandering around."

The nurse didn't bother to look up from her phone as she said, "I doubt it—she passed away last week."

"What?" Eva's voice was louder than she'd intended.

The nurse glanced up. "She was 94, honey; she's better off where she is." The nursing home served as most people's last stop on this earth, and it was normal for residents to pass away, but this was something entirely different. "Are you alright? You look like you're about to pass out."

"I... I... just really liked her." Eva hurried back to the kitchen, wondering what on earth was happening. *Nora hadn't been wandering around?* But she had seen her. She'd *talked* to her. The fluorescent lights above her flickered as she went over every detail in her head. None of it made any sense if Nora was already dead.

~

When Eva got home, the house was empty. She never enjoyed coming home to a dark house, but tonight it was creepier than normal. She let herself in and turned on all the lights. The lightbulb made a pop and went dark when she flipped it on. She shivered and toggled the light switch a couple times, but the bulb was dead. She opened the door to the backyard, and Flip shot in like a bullet, her toenails making a familiar click on the old hardwood floors. At least Flip was around. She made the empty house a little less ominous.

Eva grabbed some cookies and milk, kicked off her shoes, and sat down on the couch to do some homework. Halfway through the first question, the lights flickered and the hair on the back of her neck stood up. She peered around the room. Someone was there... someone angry. There couldn't be anyone in their tiny house though. She'd walked through each room, turning on the lights. No one was there but her and Flip.

When Eva was little, she used to get the feeling someone was with her in the room, but it was comforting. It made her less lonely. This was different. It was as if someone in the room hated her. Fear crawled over her skin like spiders. Her throat tightened with anxiety.

Get it together, Eva. Quit freaking yourself out. Do your homework and go to bed. You are fine!

But she wasn't fine. A few seconds later, she heard something clinking, metal on metal. Flip was asleep with his back against the couch, but his head popped up at the sound. He was staring at the middle of the room, whimpering as though he could see something Eva couldn't. She stood up, hands out in front of her in a defensive position.

Something sharp cut through the sleeve of Eva's t-shirt as effortlessly as a knife through warm butter. She yelped and jumped back, grabbing the first thing she laid hands on—the fire poker they'd never used. She swung it in front of her with a violence she didn't know she possessed. Fear shot through her veins when it collided with something she couldn't see. Her arm reverberated with the impact and the sound of metal on metal rang in the air. She stabbed straight forward the way knights did in the movies, and in an instant the sense of fear and darkness evaporated from the room.

Eva stood there in the silence, ears straining for the slightest sound, but it was over. She threw the poker down on the bricks in front of the fireplace and ran to her room, Flip hot on her heels. She slammed the door behind her and hopped into bed with the blankets pulled up to her eyeballs. Flip jumped up to join her on the bed.

Eva tried to calm herself with deep breaths. Her inhaler was in the bathroom and there was no way she was going out to get it. Her heart pounded loud in her ears. *What was going on?* She didn't know how much more of this she could take.

Tomorrow she was going to tell Jai'Lune everything. Maybe they could figure it out together. Maybe not. But she needed to tell *someone.* And Jai'Lune had always been her person. It would all be okay after she talked to Jai'Lune.

Chapter Four

Alex tried not to let his mind wander to the dreams—or Eva. Instead, he willed himself to focus on the burly dude in front of him talking trash about his momma. The center snapped the football and Alex's instincts took over. Neurons fired as they were conditioned to and in seconds the big guy in front of him was pancaked. The crowd roared from the metal stands and Alex put out a hand to help the guy up.

The team was full of newbies, and it was an easy win. After the game, Alex's dad came up to him and immediately started in. "You need to do a better job of shifting before the snap when they move outside like that."

Great job, Alex. Way to pancake that guy. Alex thought in frustration. Just once, it'd be nice if his dad said he did a good job. But Alex didn't have time for self-pity. If Dad thought he wasn't listening, there'd be more lectures about respect. "I gotcha. Okay, I'll work on that in practice this week. Thanks, Dad." His dad patted Alex on the back with a satisfied smile and turned to accept the praise Alex had earned from the crowd. Good, let him take it.

Dad can't help it. Alex reminded himself, the old habit of making excuses for his dad came as natural as the last football play. In the military, he'd been deployed to places where it was fight or die. Alex knew, in some convoluted place in his dad's brain, he believed being hard on his sons might save their life one day. *Who knows, maybe it will.*

All the other players were talking to friends or their girlfriends. Alex stood awkwardly holding his helmet, glancing around, and wondering what to do next. Maybe he'd slip off to the locker room and get out of the school before the crowd hit. But his mom's beaming face came out of the crowd. Whatever his dad lacked in compliments, his mom always tried to overcompensate by lavishing praise on him. "Good job, honey! That last play you really pancaked the guy. You were amazing out there."

"Thanks." Alex mustered up the most genuine smile he could. If she sensed anything was wrong, she'd hound him when they got home. *What's wrong? Is everything okay at school? With your friends? Are you still sad about Janet?* He'd been down that road. It was easier to fake happiness than talk about the truth.

"I was just heading to the locker room to beat the rush."

"Okay, okay, the showers will be there later. Let's take a few quick pictures first." It was not a request. She held up her expensive camera and Alex smiled dutifully.

Pops walked up, and Alex's heart lifted a little at his old, familiar face. Mom kept snapping pictures, but he knew it was safe to ignore her now. "Good job, champ," Pops said, throwing his arms around Alex.

Alex squeezed back. "Thanks, Pops."

"Man, those guys were huge! Number 86 was six-foot-six, 280 pounds!"

"I believe it! He felt like about three bills every time he landed on me!" Pops threw his head back and laughed. Then he slapped Alex on the back. "You up for some fishing this weekend?"

Alex looked at his mom. She shrugged. "We don't have anything going on."

"Sounds good to me! See you tomorrow." Alex was relieved to have something to look forward to. "Well, I better get showered up."

"Yep, get there before the rush. Good thinking," Pops said, with a final pat on Alex's back.

On the drive home, Alex tensed when he went past the place on the road where that strange attack happened. This time, he passed through with no issues. Maybe tomorrow while they were fishing, he could tell Pops about the weird stuff that had been happening to him lately? Pops always had answers when Alex needed help, but this was all so weird. Would he think Alex had gone crazy? Pops was the one person Alex could always be himself around. If he told Pops everything, would that change?

The dreams were coming more often now. Sometimes even two dreams a night. Then yesterday with the weird thing in his pickup. It was as if the dreams were amping up and busting into the real world. Inside Alex, unavoidable dread rose to the surface and erupted with a shudder. It was going to push him over the edge.

When Alex got home, his huge German shepherd, Trip, chased him down their long lane. When Alex opened the door, Trip jumped on him in an excited welcome. "Down, Trip," Alex said in his best stern, dad voice. Trip dropped to all fours, no doubt worried he'd get a blow to the stomach if he didn't listen, knowing the way Dad did things. Alex ruffled

Trip's ears to reassure him. Trip walked toward the house, then glanced back to see if Alex was following.

The house was dark, and Alex hoped that meant his parents had gone downtown to the local bar for a few drinks after the game. Otherwise, his dad would keep him up for another two hours going over film. It all depended on his dad's mood and tonight Alex didn't know if he could survive a late-night film session.

Alex collapsed on his bed and called for Trip to jump up. They both knew it was against the rules to have him up on the furniture, but Alex needed the company. Trip's sharp ears would catch the sound of Mom and Dad's car coming down the lane in plenty of time to hop down. Alex lay there hoping for sleep but also dreading it. The dreams were inescapable now, the price he paid for a little rest, and it almost wasn't worth it anymore. With all the sleep he'd been losing, he wondered how much more of this he could take.

Alex was running through a cornfield. The sharp leaves on the stalks cut his legs and his breath came fast but steady as he glided through the field. Alex glanced to his right and saw Eva, her graceful bare legs carrying her forward as she tried to keep up with him. Should he slow down? She was clearly exhausted. No, he needed to keep pushing them forward to safety. But from what?

Alex glanced back and saw Grace O'Donnell, red hair in a wild jumble and blue eyes large with terror. Behind her, three horrific tornados, darker than night, cut through the sky. Alex's heart pounded as he willed his body to move faster.

They reached the edge of town and ran to his church. Alex jerked the huge wooden door open and held onto it as Eva and

Grace sprinted inside. The tornados were coming fast, and he slammed the door shut behind them.

They turned in unison, realizing there were other people in the church. Familiar faces stared back at them in disapproval. Time stood still for a moment. Then Grace said, "They're coming! Take shelter. The tornados are coming!"

Alex, Eva, and Grace bolted for cover, as if setting a good example would inspire the crowd to act, but they just sat there. Alex watched in horror as one by one the people turned their back and settled into the pews, facing forward with blank stares.

Eva bolted from her hiding place and ran to the front of the church, desperately shouting to get their attention. "The tornados are coming. You need to take cover now!"

Alex's priest strutted toward Eva. His jaw was set in determination. On instinct, Alex sprang up to defend her. He saw Eva bolt in the opposite direction with surprising speed. A loud sound blared in Alex's ears, and he woke up. He was in his bedroom, not a church. It was the dreams. Again.

He rubbed the sleep from his eyes and sat up. Every muscle in his back, arms, and legs ached from the football game last night and the tension from the dreams. The smell of bacon drifted up the stairs and it gave Alex the motivation he needed to get out of bed. *You get to go fishing with Pops today.* The thought bolstered him.

Chapter Five

Eva woke up scared from another tornado dream. Flip was snoring on the floor beside her. *Some watchdog.* She flopped over, punching her pillow to fluff it. The sun was coming up, streaming through the window across from her bed, and she couldn't get back to sleep. With a huff, she threw the covers back and grabbed her computer. She wanted to know if the Bible said anything about tornado dreams.

When Eva searched *tornados or storms in the Bible* her screen sprang to life with a ton of results. Some were direct links to parts of the Bible. Others were news stories or personal blogs. She clicked on a link to a Bible passage and read:

Look! The storm of the Lord! His wrath breaks out in a whirling storm that bursts upon the heads of the wicked. The anger of the Lord will not abate until he has carried out completely the decisions of his heart. In days to come you will fully understand it. (Jeremiah 23:19-20)

Oh, that didn't sound good. Was she somehow wicked without knowing it? Is that why she was having these dreams? Was this God's way of telling her to get it together or He was going to strike her down?

At least it said, in days to come you will fully understand it. But when would the "days to come" actually come? She needed to understand what was going on now. She clicked back and found another Bible verse.

"These people are waterless springs and mists driven by a gale; for them the gloom of darkness has been reserved." (2 Peter 2:17)

Darkness? Eva shivered and clicked the back button. Scanning the results chose another. It said, *"And suddenly a great wind came from across the desert and smashed the four corners of the house. It fell upon the young people and they are dead; I alone have escaped to tell you." (Job 1:19)*

Eva cringed and peered up at her ceiling, imagining it crashing down. Should she be digging a bomb shelter or something? No, that's what crazy people did, right? Dig a shelter and buy too much canned food.

She was getting too wrapped up in this. Eva wasn't sure what she believed about God, but one thing she knew for sure, He wouldn't waste time sending a nobody like her special messages. There had to be another explanation for all this.

Maybe her subconscious was trying to tell her something? She typed 'symbolism of a tornado' into the search engine and read through the results. They all said tornados meant you had great upheaval in your life. Upheaval no, boredom yes. Scratch that.

Eva felt frustrated. One more try, then she'd be done. She clicked on another link, and it brought up a short post with a video. The preview to the video was a pretty blonde girl with tired, dark circles under her eyes. She was frozen beside a dark-haired girl with her lips pressed together, staring intently at Eva from the screen. The information below said they were from California and the title of the video was *Tornado Dreams and a Search for Answers*. She clicked the link, her hands tingling.

The video sprang to life. The dark-haired girl talked as though she were imitating a news anchor's voice. "This is Monica Force with Blogging Truth, here today with Samantha Firth, a girl who needs answers. How are you today, Samantha?"

"I'm okay, thanks."

"You say you've been having some strange dreams, and you don't know what they mean. Can you tell us more about that?"

Eva held her breath, waiting for the girl's next words. "Yes, they always start a little different, and I'm in a new place each time. But in all the dreams, there are these three black, menacing tornados. I try to warn people the tornados are coming, but no one will listen to me. That's when I wake up... right before the tornados hit."

"Well, there you have it, folks. We're in the business of helping people find the truth. If there is anyone out there who might know what these dreams mean, leave a note for us in the comments below."

Eva glanced up at her lights, which flickered several times as the video wrapped up. She sat there in awe, too shocked to move or click anywhere else. How was someone hundreds of miles away having the same dreams as her? Finally, she scrolled down. Maybe this was her chance to find some answers.

There were a bunch of stupid, *oh man, that's crazy,* comments. Someone named RachaelRun left a comment dated two months ago, which Eva realized was about the time she'd started having her dreams. It said: *Yep, that's pretty much what my dreams are like. Will someone please tell me what this means?*

Another comment from Amber3000 said: *It sounds like evil spirits tormenting your dreams. They always cause chaos and fear.*

CatholicMom9 commented: *Sounds like a warning to me.*

Not sure what the tornados mean, but that's what you need to find out. The number three signifies completion. Maybe it's the darkness the saints have been predicting?

Mombo12 left a link: *Here's more information on what CatholicMom9 is talking about.*

Eva's curiosity got the better of her, and she clicked on the link. It took her to a website in maroon and gold tones with a picture of Jesus at the top. In the middle, it said, *for hundreds of years, prophets from all over the world have been receiving warnings. Despite living in different times and places, they all have the same chilling message—a time of three days of darkness is coming. Those who love God must go to their inner rooms and pray God's angels will be strong for battle.*

Eva shivered and scrolled down to what appeared to be a Bible verse: *Finally, draw your strength from the Lord and from his mighty power. Put on the armor of God so that you may be able to stand firm against the tactics of the devil. For our struggle is not with flesh and blood but with the principalities, with the powers, with the world rulers of this present darkness, with the evil spirits in the heavens. Therefore, put on the armor of God, that you may be able to resist on the evil day and, having done everything, to hold your ground. (Ephesians 6:10-13, NABRE)*

Below that were quotes and Eva scrolled down quickly, intrigued now. *All the light in the world will be gone. The only light will come from blessed candles. The faithful—those who have embraced the love of God—must go into their homes and light their blessed candles. Those who have rejected God's love will be forced to wander in darkness and fear. The true darkness of life without God revealed, as the demons wreak havoc on the earth. On the third day, the candles will go out and the sun will come back. Be ready, my children. Be ready. (Mystic vision of Saint Ferdinadito, Brazil AD 800.)*

During the time of darkness, go into your house. Close the doors and windows, and do not look outside. For a terrible battle is being waged between God's holy angels and the demons of the abyss. The poor souls who have rejected God's love will have no protection from the torments of the darkness. (Mystic vision of Saint Antonio, Italy AD 1200.)

Eva slammed her laptop shut. Why was the internet full of creeps and weirdos? Her mom always said Catholics were crazy. What did this have to do with her dreams, anyhow? She'd gotten off track, taken it too far. She couldn't think about it anymore or it was going to drive her nuts. Her phone rang, making her jump. It was Jai'Lune. "Hello?"

"You okay?"

"Yeah."

"You don't sound okay."

"I'm fine. What's up?"

"Some people are going to the lake, and I wanna go. Please say you'll come with me?"

"Grace mentioned something about that."

"Grace?"

"Yeah, we were partners in math."

"Oh, okay. Do you want to go? I'll drive."

Eva considered her options. Sit around the house creeping herself out about these stupid dreams all day or go have some fun in the sun. "Sure, I'll go. What time?"

"Really? Great! Right after lunch. I'll pick you up. Woo-hoo!"

Eva dug through her drawers for her swimsuit and put it on under her shorts and t-shirt. *Maybe the dreams would stop.* They were random anyway—a bunch of neurons firing.

Something tugged at her mind. *Then why are other people having them, too?* Maybe they all watched the same video and somehow it messed with their brains and triggered the dreams. There had to be a logical explanation.

Eva got a bag ready with a towel and sunscreen, then

opened the fridge to make a bologna sandwich. A six-pack of beer was staring her in the face. Who knew how long it'd been in there. No doubt her mom forgot they even had it. She could take it, and no one would know. Other people would probably drink at the lake. At least she'd blend in. She shook her head and slammed the refrigerator door shut. She wasn't that person.

She made a sandwich and ate it outside on her tire swing, dragging her feet in the dirt and trying not to think about the dreams. Soon Jai'Lune pulled up, and Eva hopped in. "Hey!"

"Hey! We have to pick up Vanessa too."

Eva rolled her eyes, then glanced at Jai'Lune, hoping she didn't notice. "Okay," she said. Eva wanted to talk to Jai'Lune about the dreams on the way out to the lake, but now that wouldn't happen. Vanessa was one of those girls who floated from group to group—friends with everyone, loyal to no one. She was okay to hang out with, but the last thing you wanted to do was tell Vanessa your secrets.

Jai'Lune glanced sideways at Eva as she backed out of the driveway. "Come on, Eva, don't be like that! Vanessa is the one who told me about the party. We can't ditch her."

How did she always know what Eva was thinking? "I know. It's fine," Eva said, trying to sound believable.

Chapter Six

Alex was smart enough to know he'd been invited to the lake party by accident. Or maybe by obligation. He had walked into the locker room when the guys were talking about it and, like an idiot, he had said, "Oh, you're going to the gravel pit lake? There's good fishing there."

Collin laughed in that easy way of his. "Ha, good fishing for chicks in bikinis, maybe. You should come, bro. Get back out there. Show Janet you're not sitting around missing her."

Before he knew what he was saying, he'd agreed to go. What was he thinking? People would no doubt be drinking. Dad would kill him if they got busted and Coach benched him. But he had to admit it was nice to be invited to something—even if it was by accident. He had decided it wouldn't hurt anything to make a quick appearance, check it out, and get the heck out of there.

Now that he was here, he wondered if he made the right decision. But he forced himself to walk up to a group of football players standing in a circle talking, and Collin slapped him on the shoulder. "Bro, you came! Want a beer?"

"Um, no I'm good."

At that, someone in the group said, "What? You too good to have a few drinks? Or you here so you can narc on us later?"

The blood rushed to his face. "No! I wouldn't do that!" The last thing he wanted was for half the linemen to get benched.

Collin laughed and gave him that familiar *you are a real weirdo* smile. "Relax, he was joking."

Maybe he should go. What was he even doing here? But then he saw *her* come over the edge of the dune. Eva seemed as uncomfortable as he was as she squinted into the sun, scanning the crowd. *Who's she searching for?* He wondered.

Eva slipped a few feet on the loose gravel, and he realized he was holding his breath. *Don't fall.* In a small town, falling down a dune at a party could get you a nasty nickname for life. She kept herself upright. Good for her.

Collin waved to Jai'Lune, and the girls headed their way. Collin popped out of the group to talk to Jai'Lune. He had a huge smile on his face. *Did Collin have a crush on Jai'Lune?* Weird. Jai'Lune was not the kind of girl Alex thought Collin would go after. She was... unique. Not like any of the other girls in their class. Maybe he didn't know Collin as well as he thought.

Collin held out a beer for each of them. It surprised Alex when Eva took one, but he noticed she didn't even bother to open it. Jai'Lune waved the beer away with a smile and an eye roll. Vanessa said, "I'll take hers!" and grabbed both beers.

Eva was laying her towel out on the dirty sand and Alex saw his chance. Someone to talk to. And not just someone, *Eva*. "Is this seat taken?" He plopped down on the sand beside her towel.

"Um, no? Guess not."

"I didn't expect to see you here," he said, trying for an easy smile.

"I didn't expect to see myself here either." She shrugged.

Okay. Now what? He panicked. He hadn't thought this one through. A breeze hit his face, the smell of lake water and sunscreen mixed, carrying with it the memory of summer. "Uh, how was your summer?" He blurted.

"Fine. I worked a lot." Eva perched on her towel, and he wondered if she was questioning her decision to come too. Should he leave her alone and go already?

But then she asked him, "How was your summer?"

Internally, he sighed with relief before searching for an answer that wasn't lame. "It was okay. I did a bunch of camps for football and wrestling and stuff. Weightlifting." He shrugged. If only he could lift his way to a few more inches of height. He was taller than Eva, though. That was something.

She peered at him like he was a weirdo and he realized he'd been spacing. Uh-oh, did she say something to him? "What?"

"I said, do you enjoy doing all that stuff? The camps and lifting?"

"It's okay. It's all a part of it, you know? I like to be active." It helped with his ADHD. If he worked his body hard enough each day, he didn't get that antsy sensation like he was going to jump out of his own skin. "Sometimes I miss the old days, though, you know? Spending the entire summer doing whatever I wanted. Going to the pool. Staying at my grandparents." *Climbing a tree and sitting in the branches, reading for hours.* But he didn't want to sound weird, so he kept that part to himself.

"Your grandpa lives on the farm next to my grandparents, right?" She asked.

"Um, yeah, I think so. It's on the south edge of town. Has that stream that runs through the pasture."

"Yep. I ride my horses down there with Gramps sometimes."

"That's cool."

"Yep."

Alex peered out at the lake sparkling in the sunlight. "Uh, you wanna go take a dip in the lake? It's getting kinda hot." What was he doing? Get out of there, man! Bail, bail.

"Um, okay. I guess." Eva stood up and tugged off the shirt she was wearing over her swimsuit. The action mesmerized Alex and as the shirt cleared her head, she caught him staring. Not sure what to say, he turned and walked toward the water. He glanced over his shoulder, and to his relief, she was following.

The water lapped against his body, cooling him and little pebbles shifted under his feet as he waded out deeper. He stopped when the water was waist high, and Eva caught up with him.

She twirled around in a full circle. "I forgot this used to be a gravel pit. Can you imagine a bunch of equipment sitting around scooping out gravel? Now it's beautiful and serene."

"Yea, crazy," he said, wishing he could come up with something more intelligent to say. But she seemed too lost in her own imagination to notice.

"What do you do for fun, Eva?" Alex asked.

Her eyes refocused on his face. "I don't know. Read, I guess. How about you?"

"Yea, I read a lot." Her stunned face made him blurt, "And go fishing with my grandpa." Hopefully that sounded cooler than reading.

"Sounds nice. What do you read?"

"Action. Fantasy. That kind of stuff. You?"

"Mostly historical fiction."

"Nice."

"Where do you go fishing?"

"Sometimes in that stream that goes through the farm when the water's high. Or the pond in another pasture. Pops keeps it stocked. We can catch some big catfish on a good day. We call the biggest one we ever caught gargantuan. He evaded us for five years, but we finally got him." *Gosh, tell her your entire life story.*

But to his surprise, she laughed. "Do you eat them?"

"The fish? No. Mom won't let us. She's afraid farming chemicals or something nasty might be in the pond."

"Oh." Eva nodded, as if that explained it all.

Alex let himself fall backward, and the weight of his body pulled him under the water. He stood up, smoothing the water out of his hair, and realized Eva was staring at him with her mouth open. She blushed and turned her head away, gazing off into the distance. After a moment, she said, "I heard you and Janet broke up. Again."

Janet. How did he keep making that mistake over and over? But he had to admit, crazy as she was, in some ways Janet had made his life easier. She'd asked *him* out. She'd kept the conversation going, so he didn't have to work as hard at it. His mom thought she was great, too. Not to mention she was pretty. It was easier to let inertia take over and date her. But she was bossy and so jealous one time she even freaked out when he spent all weekend with his cousins from out of town.

Alex realized Eva was waiting for an answer. With a nervous chuckle, he said, "Yeah, I guess I'm a slow learner. But this time was the last time."

"Well, the feeling wasn't mutual. If looks could kill, we'd both be dead right now."

He grimaced and snuck a glance over Eva's shoulder at Janet. She was staring daggers at them. When he shifted his attention back to Eva, he noticed her fair skin was turning an angry shade of pink. "Oh man, you're burning."

Eva glanced down at her arms and sighed. "Stupid pale skin. I forgot to put on sunscreen." Without another word, she turned and trudged back to shore. Just like that, their little oasis was over.

Alex was right behind Eva, trudging across the beach

toward her towel, when suddenly she yelped and grabbed her foot. "Ouch!" He could see bright red blood oozing from the pad of her foot.

A glint of green caught the sunlight. "Oh man! There's glass in the sand." Alex scooped her off the ground. She blushed ten shades of red and people stopped talking and turned their attention to them. He'd acted on instinct, so she didn't step on anything else, and he was committed now. He ignored their stares and carried her to her towel.

Alex carefully set Eva down and the blood seeped into the cotton towel in a small circle. Alex was unsure what to do next.

"Oh, that stinks," someone said from behind them. Eva and Alex turned to see Grace walking up in her bikini. Her perfume danced in the air as she knelt beside Eva. "I grabbed the little brats swim bag by accident. I think I saw some Band-Aids in there. I'll grab you one."

"I'll go get a bottle of water to rinse it," Alex offered, and turned to go find the cooler he'd brought. He grabbed a water and jogged back to her. "Here you go."

"Thanks." She didn't look at him. *Had he done something wrong?* Eva poured the water over her cut and dried it off with her towel. The bleeding had almost stopped.

He plopped down on the sand next to her. Grace returned with a Band-Aid, ripped it open and stuck it over Eva's cut in one practiced motion. "Thanks." Eva gave Grace a wobbly smile, and Alex realized she was embarrassed.

"Of course! What are friends for?"

Alex hadn't realized Grace and Eva were friends. But he remembered they'd both been in his dream. Maybe on a subconscious level, he somehow knew. The memory of the dreams made his stomach flip, and he was ready to go. He'd experienced enough of the party for one day.

Chapter Seven

Friends? Is that what they were? First Alex, now Grace—sunshine made people do strange things. Why was Alex talking to her anyhow? Maybe it was a ploy to make Janet jealous. She didn't appreciate being a pawn in the ongoing Janet and Alex saga.

But then Eva noticed the droplets of water dancing in the sunlight on Alex's tan skin. She couldn't help but remember the way he'd scooped her up out of the sand, his firm chest pressed up against her. Something about being that close to him made her dizzy. *It was probably all the blood loss.*

She couldn't help but notice he'd put on at least ten pounds of muscle over the summer. His well-defined arms were golden from the sun and his calf muscles jutted out like it was their job to announce to the world how fast he was. Eva realized she was staring and glanced away, hoping he didn't notice. Thank God for sunglasses. *Get it together Eva!*

Jai'Lune jogged over. "Hey, you okay? Somebody said you were bleeding."

"Yeah, you know me—super lucky. I stepped on some glass in the sand."

"Is it bad?"

"No, it already stopped bleeding."

"Oh, good." She sounded relieved.

Eva spotted some outhouses down the beach, and she was already regretting the soda she'd chugged on the way over. "I'm gonna run to the bathroom. Be right back."

"I'll come with you," Grace said, jumping up to walk beside Eva. "I need to go too."

"Uh, okay," Eva said, not doing well at hiding her surprise.

"Are you having fun?" Grace said as Eva tried not to limp beside her. "I've never seen you at the lake before."

"Yeah, I work a lot. I'm having fun, though." Eva was surprised to realize she meant it. Despite the gash on her foot and the death glare from Janet, it had been a good time.

"Good! I almost didn't come because I've been so tired lately. Think I could have slept straight through until Monday."

"Me too. I fell asleep halfway through a math problem the other day. I mean, it's boring, but still."

"Oh my gosh, I've never done that before, but I'm tired enough I think I could. Why have you been so tired?"

Eva glanced at her, wondering if she should mention the dreams. Her first thought was no, but why not? People had dreams all the time, right? She didn't have to make it sound like a big deal. "Oh, I've been having these stupid dreams that keep waking me up."

"Really?" She sounded intrigued. "What kind of dreams?"

Now Eva wished she'd kept her mouth shut. "Oh, there just... there are these tornados, and I'm running around, trying to warn everyone."

"... but no one will listen," Grace and Eva finished the sentence at the same time.

Eva stopped walking and stared at Grace. "How did you know that?"

"Because I'm having the same dreams."

Eva's skin crawled. "What?"

"I'm serious. There're always these three nasty tornados, but the people and the places are different. I've been trying to figure out what they mean."

"Me too," Eva admitted. "Have you found anything?"

"Not really. You?"

"No, well, maybe? I found some stuff online, but it wasn't that helpful."

"What did it say?" her voice was hushed and conspiratorial as she leaned toward Eva.

Eva told her what she'd read about the darkness coming.

"I've heard my Great Granny talk about that! She said if we're not careful, we're gonna get sucked into darkness or something." Grace shivered. "It always creeps me out when she talks about it, and I try to change the subject. So, I don't know anything else."

"The whole thing is creepy. I can send you the link," Eva offered, forgetting for a moment she was talking to one of the most popular girls at school.

"That'd be good. We're going to Granny's house tomorrow. I'll see if I can get her talking about it. I hope she doesn't notice my sudden interest and get suspicious. Granny always knows when something's up." Grace smiled, but it didn't quite make it to her eyes.

"I'm hoping someday the dreams will just go away."

Grace nodded, "Me too. I don't know how much longer I can handle being this tired."

~

Why was getting out of bed in the morning such a monumental task? Eva's head was pounding, her mouth was dry, and her foot was killing her where she'd stepped on the glass. She pulled her foot out from under the covers and squinted at it.

The cut was red around the edges, but smaller. Good. The last thing she needed was to go to the doctor, or worse yet... tell Mom where she'd been when it happened. Eva swung her legs over the edge of the bed and stood up, careful not to put too much weight on her right foot as she walked to the bathroom.

Eva always met Gram and Gramps at Ellie's Café after they went to church on Sunday mornings, and she didn't want to be late. Her mom joined them when she wasn't working, and Eva was hoping she'd be there today. She could use some time with her.

Eva dressed and peeked into her mom's bedroom, but the light was off. Her heart sank. But she shoved the loneliness down with a practiced motion and did her best to ignore it. The smell of coffee hit her, and her heart lifted when she walked in the kitchen and saw her mom standing at the counter with her back to Eva. "Hey, Mom!"

"Morning." Her mom didn't bother to turn around.

"What're you doing up this early? Are you gonna go to breakfast with us?" Eva cringed at the hope she'd let creep into her voice. The last thing she wanted was to make her mom feel guilty for working her butt off to support them.

"Sorry, honey, I can't. I picked up an extra shift at the gas station. But swing by there afterward and say hi, okay?"

"Sure." Eva hid the disappointment as best she could.

"See you later." Rachel paused to kiss Eva on the forehead as she walked by. Eva closed her eyes to soak up the moment, but the screen door made her jump as it slammed behind her mom on the way out.

~

When Eva got to Ellie's Café, the typical Sunday brunch crowd was there. Mike and Tom, the sixty-year-old identical twin farmers you never saw apart. Millie, who'd been a widow for a couple of decades, her weird little dog on the bench beside her. Dutiful adult children sitting across from her, eyes glazed over. The 70-year-old-plus crowd of gray hairs at the big circle table were smiling and carrying on multiple conversations at once while they sipped their coffee.

Eva put a polite smile on her face as she walked past the tables with their mix-matched vinyl tablecloths. The menus sat propped between glass ketchup bottles and silver napkin holders for the newbies passing through town. All the locals knew their options by heart.

Gramps and Gram were waiting for Eva at their usual table, a hot cup of coffee steaming at her place. She leaned down and hugged both of them before taking a seat.

"How are you, honey?" Gram sounded as though she truly wanted to know. "You're limping a little. What's wrong?"

"I'm fine," Eva said with a sigh. "I cut my foot on a little glass, but it's no big deal."

Gram worked as a nurse for forty years. She probably knew more than some doctors by now, and their family always counted on her for medical advice. It had saved Eva plenty of doctor visits growing up, which was lucky. But right now, she didn't want to explain how she hurt her foot, and she was pathetic at lying. Gram would see right through her.

Eva held her breath as she waited for Gram's next words. Would she demand Eva take her shoe and sock off right there in the middle of the café to inspect her foot? Eva let out her breath when Gram said, "Okay, well, if it gets red or oozes, you call me. You hear?"

"Yes ma'am. How was church?" Anything to change the subject.

"Great, as always. You know you're always welcome to come." Gram invited Eva for the millionth time. "We could pick you up right along the way."

Before Eva could form yet another nice thanks but no thanks, Gramps chimed in, "Yeah, Father kept the sermon to ten minutes this time. I'm liking this new guy. That last feller took forever. By the time we got outta there, my stomach was always howling like a tomcat for lunch."

"Oh, John, stop!" Gram gave his arm a light pat. It was an ongoing joke, loosely disguised as a quibble that had probably been going on since the day they got married sixty years ago. Eva sure admired their stick-with-it-ness. She couldn't imagine being in a relationship for that long. She knew things weren't always easy, especially when her uncle got cancer as a little kid and died. They never gave up on each other, though. Stuck with it through thick and thin. Maybe someday she would find someone who would do the same.

Ellie came over, apron on and pitcher of ice water in hand. "Let me guess, Miss Eva... eggs and waffles?" Eva smiled. All the locals had their favorite food they ate every time they came in and Ellie had them all memorized. But Eva was different. She tried to never order the same thing twice in a row to keep it interesting. Ever since she was small, Ellie had made a game of guessing what she would order. "Close! Eggs and bacon please. Oh, and a chocolate chip muffin."

"Um-em, child. Where do you put all that food? Skinny little thing." Ellie turned and walked away. She tossed over her shoulder, "The usual for you two?"

Eva's grandparents chuckled. "Yes, ma'am, thank you."

Mrs. Cotner walked up and put her arm on Gram's shoulder. "Wanda, I heard he's back in town. How you doing?"

"Fine. We're fine. It doesn't impact us." Gram lifted her chin a little. Eva could see the irritation in Gram's eyes, but Mrs. Cotner didn't appear to notice. Or more likely didn't care. She wanted answers that would give her something to gossip about.

Mrs. Cotner patted Gram's shoulder. "Well, you let me know if you need anything. I don't know how he can show his face after what he did."

"Thanks." Gram turned her back to the woman, dismissing her.

Mrs. Cotner took the hint and shuffled off to the cash register to pay her bill, no doubt in one-dollar bills and without leaving a tip. Gram's strong reaction to the woman's questions made Eva curious. "Who's back in town, Gram?" *And why do you care so much?*

"Never mind, honey. We'll talk about it later."

"Okay, but now I'm curious, Gram. Can't you just tell me quick? Then we'll talk about it later?" Eva didn't care if she was being a whiny five-year-old. There was a pit of dread in her stomach. "Please," she whispered.

Gram sighed. "Well, I didn't want to tell you this way, sweetheart, but I suppose it's better you hear it from me than someone else." She put a comforting hand on my arm. "Honey, it's your father, Russell. He moved back to town."

All the wind rushed out of Eva's chest. "My . . . father?" she managed, her voice scratchy and the words foreign in her mouth.

"Now control your breathing, Eva, or you're going to have another one of your asthma attacks. In and out. That's it. Do you have your inhaler on you?"

Eva never went anywhere without it. "Yes, but I'm okay." Most of what she knew about Russell was gleaned from adult conversations and rude comments. Apparently, he'd gotten her mom pregnant when they were both in high school. His mom sent him to live with his dad, and he never came back.

He never sent birthday cards or tried to contact Eva. She'd always assumed she was one of the many mistakes he'd made in life. She knew he'd never come back for *her*. Who would come back for a mistake? He must be here for some other reason. But what?

Gram's full attention was trained on Eva's face. Her breathing. Her expressions as she watched Eva process the news.

Ellie walked up with their plates and must have sensed the somber mood at the table. "Here you go, hun." She set a plate of food in front of Eva, but she'd lost her appetite. Eva stared down at her hands resting in her lap, willing the tears to go away. Hoping Ellie didn't notice. Thank God for Gram making polite conversation. Eva didn't want to cry. Not here. Not in front of Gramps and Gram. She was mad at herself. Why did she care this much about someone coming to town who obviously didn't care about her?

When Ellie left, Gram turned her attention back to Eva. "I wouldn't worry about it too much, honey. Let it be and see what happens. Chances are he won't stay long. Men like that don't. He'll probably leave soon, and we can all get on with our lives." Eva had a haunting feeling Gram had spoken those words before. Gramps sat there eating quietly. He'd never been one for strong emotions.

Eva tried to push down the tidal wave of emotions rushing over her. To numb herself the way she had when she missed her mom all those lonely nights at home. But this was different. This pain was deeper, hidden in some secret place inside her she hadn't even known existed until now, sitting at Ellie's diner. She had to get out. She needed space. To be in the open air. "I think... I'm gonna head home."

"We all will," Gram said. Gramps shoved another bite in his mouth and dutifully got up to pay the bill.

As they walked out Gramps said, "Why don't you come by the house this afternoon? We'll take Bessy and Billy out for a ride. They ain't been rode in a while. It'll be good for them."

Eva didn't want to go anywhere. She wanted to curl up on her bed and cry away all these feelings. But she didn't have the heart to say no to Gramps. "Okay, I will."

The moment Eva walked in her front door, she remembered her mom's invitation to stop by the gas station. Well, that wasn't happening right now. She'd break down bawling the minute she saw her mom and the last thing either of them wanted was to make a public scene.

Did mom know Russell was back? The thought hit her hard. If her mom didn't know, she would soon. Eva groaned. She wasn't going to be the one to tell her. She wondered what it would do to her mom after all these years. She had her life together. Their life together. Would it all come crashing down?

Eva let Flip into the house to keep her company, then flopped down on her bed, letting the tears pour out. She jolted awake and peered around, confused at the bright sunlight pouring into her room from the window. All the memories came rushing back and her heart sank. She must have cried herself to sleep. *What time was it?* Remembering her promise to Gramps, she grabbed her phone. It was only 1:30. Plenty of time, she sighed.

Eva forced herself out of bed and splashed some cold water on her face. She checked her reflection in the mirror. She needed to swing by the gas station on her way to Gramp's and Gram's. Hopefully, her mom wouldn't notice she'd been crying. When she got to the gas station, her mom was helping someone else, so she grabbed a candy bar and a soda before heading to the cash register. "Hey, Mom."

"Well, hello there! I thought you forgot about me," her mom said, a surprised smile spreading across her face.

"Sorry, I fell asleep after breakfast and didn't make it over. I'm headed out to ride Bessy and Billy with Gramps."

"Well, that sounds fun. Why do you look like something the cat dragged in?"

"I'm still waking up."

She nodded, happy to accept the explanation. For as long as Eva could remember, she and her mom had an unspoken agreement. She didn't make any trouble for her mom, and her mom gave her total freedom and a place to sleep and eat. Maybe it wasn't ideal, especially when Eva had been six, but it worked for them. It was survival. "Okay, well, you have a good time, and be nice to old Bessy. She was my first horse, you know."

"I know. I know." Eva heard all about it from Gramps on their many, many rides.

Chapter Eight

As Eva walked through the front door at Gramp's and Gram's, Gramps said, "Oh, hey there kiddo, perfect timing. I was just getting ready to head to the barn." He grabbed his old hat off the peg by the door. She was pretty sure that hat had been around longer than she had. Gramps was a farmer, like his parents and grandparents were before him, and his legs bowed from years of riding horses, but he still could get around well.

Eva fell into step beside him, grateful with Gramps there was no need to fill the silence with conversation. They worked together to saddle up Bessy and Billy. Each talked only when necessary as they swung the woven blankets on the horses' backs, set the heavy leather saddles on top and cinched the straps underneath.

Eva took a deep breath of the earthy barn smells. As she did, the tension in her shoulders eased a bit. The piles of hay reminded her of hours spent playing with Jai'Lune in the barn when they were young. They'd create magical worlds and Jai'Lune would tell the most epic stories about battling horrible beasts. She marveled at the vivid imagination Jai'Lune had even as a young child.

Eva and Gramps led the horses out of the barn. Gramps held Billy's reins and Eva held Bessy's. For as long as she could remember, the horses had been old and gentle. She and Gramps took them out for frequent rides when she was younger, but it'd been a while since they'd gone. She wondered if Gramps would have a hard time getting up in the saddle. It would hurt his pride if she offered to help. She hopped on her mare, turning her back to give Gramps some privacy to get into the saddle however he could.

To her surprise, he rode up beside her moments later with a wide grin. "Man, it's good to be back in the saddle again." He hummed a few notes to a song. "Where to, kiddo?"

"How about the creek?" It had always been her favorite trail. They turned their horses in that direction, and Eva mapped out the path in her mind. They'd go through the pasture to the creek, down five miles, cross the creek at a shallow part, and make a loop back around across the bridge to Gramp's house.

"Well, Eva, I'm going to get right to it before I chicken out. I had a double meaning inviting you along on this ride today." She glanced at him, surprised but not saying anything.

"I know your mom and grandma don't think it's right you should know the story a what happened with your dad, but I think that's horse poop. You're old enough now, and with your dad being back in town, it's time you knew."

Eva's mouth went dry. *This again?* She was trying to forget their disturbing little brunch news. But Gramps didn't talk much. If he was saying something, she knew it was worth listening. She nodded for him to continue because she didn't trust her voice.

"Your mom and dad dated all through high school. Russell

always joked they would have dated in elementary if he could have worked up the nerve to ask her. You could tell they adored each other. None of that annoying young puppy love stuff. From the get-go, they were real sincere and grown up about it. They respected each other and your dad thought your mom could walk on water. Adored her, you see?"

He glanced over as if to gauge her reaction. Eva was staring straight ahead, her teeth clenched to keep her emotions in check. He went on, "Well, then your mom got pregnant her senior year. I guess we shoulda seen it coming, but there're some things you're blind to when it's your own kid."

"Course, her being pregnant was a big scandal back then, what with us being church folk and all. Truth be told, I think Russell's mom woulda liked to have things taken care of, if you know what I mean." He blushed a little, but Eva got his drift and nodded, hoping he'd go on.

"Well, that made Russell real mad, and he fought with his mom a whole heap. The stress of it all weighed real heavy on everyone, and your mom and dad's relationship felt the strain. In the end, Russell's mom said she wasn't gonna have no baby screwing up her son's life. She worked too hard for that to happen and so on and so forth. She sent Russell away to live with his dad up north in Rock Rapids.

"Your daddy was real broke up about being that far from your mom, especially with the baby. Well, with you, I guess you could say, on the way. His father was a no-good drunk. Hardly had a pot to pee in. Definitely not enough money for Russell to go gallivanting off to see your mom very often. To get himself by between visits, Russell took up drinking just like his daddy.

"He was a good kid, that one. Don't you be getting me wrong, thinking I didn't like the boy. Coulda tanned his hide after what he went and done to your mom, getting her pregnant, but that there's another story altogether." It surprised Eva to hear Gramps didn't hate Russell. She'd taken it for granted that he felt the same as the rest of her family.

"Russell went on drinking. His daddy not paying him no never mind, and all the beer he could want right there in the fridge. The one time your mom went up to see him, she was beaming with excitement. She was going to surprise him. But when she got there, he was drunk as a skunk, and they had a big fight. She told him 'How could you ever be a good father if you're gonna drink like a fish,' and so on and so forth. She ended the relationship." Gramps waved his hand, then chopped the air with finality.

"Your mom came back from that trip crying buckets. Told us what happened. It took weeks to get her calmed back down. As the world goes, along comes you, pretty as the sunshine on a winter day. The apple of all our eyes.

"Now, mind you, your mom was still in school. When you was about one month old, your daddy came back to town. He'd turned nineteen and had the freedom to make his own choices. He begged your mom to take him back, and I thought she was gonna do it. Truth be told, I half hoped she would. Gram and I weren't much older than that when we started our family. We knew it could be done, and I'd seen the love those kids had for each other."

Gramp's horse stopped to eat some grass. He tugged on the reins, giving Billy a little pressure in the ribs to get him walking again. "But something hardened in your mom on that trip up to see your daddy, and I ain't never seen it soften since. She told Russell she was perfectly capable of taking care of you on her own, and he could get himself on outta town and never come back.

"Your daddy, now, he tried to change her mind, but she wouldn't budge. Gram stood behind your mom, saying drunks never change. No doubt she helped slam the door in his face. Course I don't know what's been happening with Russell since then. Never heard hide nor hair from him all these years, but I'll tell you, if I had to guess, I'd say he's back in town because a you."

The tears Eva had worked hard to hold back broke through and traced their way down her cheeks. She turned her head away from Gramps, focusing on the distant horizon as she tried to get herself together.

Gramps paused for a long while before he spoke again. "I'm sorry, sweetheart. I know it's hard, but you gotta right to know. A daddy's a real important part of a child's life, and I don't want you going and getting poisoned to him on accountta what other people think. You make up your own mind about him, you hear? Don't let no one tell you what you think about your own flesh and blood. Can't nobody make that decision for you."

Eva's throat was tight from holding back a sob. After a long pause, she managed to say, "Okay Gramps."

"There'll be heck to pay if your mom and Gram find out I told you everything. But we brushed this under the rug once and that ended terrible. Maybe there's another way this time."

Eva nodded, playing back the details of his story in her mind. Gramps said her mom had hardened something inside her. Couldn't Eva tell the exact same thing was happening inside her at the café? You had to harden and seal things up or you'd break to bits. Maybe Gramps was right though, and she shouldn't build walls. Maybe there was another way.

Gramps and Eva didn't talk much the rest of the ride. The birds chirped on, oblivious that her world had been shaken to its core. The familiar, steady thump of Bessie's feet on the soft earth was the background noise to her racing thoughts. Her mind was a million miles away, and the smell of the pasture barely reached her nose.

When they got back to the barn, Eva slid off Bessie and hugged Gramps. "Thanks for telling me."

He hugged her back. "You bet, sweetheart. It'll all be okay. I promise."

On Monday, Eva was running late to school and grateful her first hour teacher always rolled in about ten minutes late. Eva wouldn't get a tardy if she could beat her to school. The hallways were empty when she got there. She stepped into the classroom and Jai'Lune shook her finger, pretending to scold her. "You're late! I thought you weren't coming. What's the matter? Too much fun in the sun with Sir Alex Hottie Pants?"

Eva tried to give Jai'Lune the *You're crazy* look, but her face flushed red betraying her. "No! Shhh. What?" Jai'Lune could be so loud sometimes. Eva glanced around to see if anyone else heard her.

"Oh, honey, thanks to Janet's tirade, everybody is already talking about it. I guess after we left, she was screaming about how Alex was a cheating jerk, and he'd probably been with you all along. Said she saw how he looked at you, and she knew what was going on."

Eva's eyes got big. "Are you kidding me? Jai'Lune, if you are messing with me right now, I swear I'll..."

"Would I kid about something this important?" She held up her hands to profess her innocence. Then she eyed Eva with suspicion. "I didn't even know you *liked* him! What *else* aren't you telling me?"

"I didn't . . . I mean, I don't."

"You don't what?"

"We talked for two seconds at the lake. I cut my foot like an idiot, and it was over. He left. That's it."

“Well, that’s not what everybody else thought, and Janet is all worked up about it.”

Eva sank down in her chair. “Great.” She didn’t need more drama in her life. It was bad enough she was dealing with the stupid dreams and her dad back in town. Now this? She spent the rest of the day dodging Janet in the hallway and evading curious questions about her and Alex. *As if there was such a thing!*

Chapter Nine

Alex couldn't stop thinking about Eva. There was something different about her. He loved the shy way she looked at him and how she could carry on a conversation about more than her weekend plans or the latest gossip. How had Alex never noticed her before?

He wanted to ask her out and spend more time with her. He even wrote his phone number on a tiny piece of notebook paper and carried it around with him all week. But he couldn't work up the nerve to ask her out. *Was it too soon after Janet?* He didn't want Eva to be a rebound. She deserved much more than that. Now it was Friday, and he was running out of time. He needed to do it already.

Alex spotted Eva making her mad dash for home. Man, that girl was fast. He jogged to catch up with her. "You don't waste any time getting out of here, do you?"

"Nope!" She wasn't slowing down for him either, as he fell into step beside her.

"Sorry about all the craziness with Janet this week. She has a way of making other people's lives more difficult." *Why did he bring up Janet?* Maybe he should bail before he screwed up anymore. He didn't have to do this. *No.* Somehow, he did.

"It's okay. I guess I don't see what the big deal is, you know? We're not even a thing. We talked once at the lake."

"It was nice though. The talking, I mean. We should try it again."

"What, talking? I talk every day. We're talking right now."

"No, I mean go on a date or hang out or whatever." *Smooth bro.*

Eva stopped walking. Alex stopped too. "What is this?" She waved her arms and the anger in her voice caught Alex off guard. "Some kind of prank?" She peered around. "Are your friends hiding behind the trees, videoing this so you can share it and get a few laughs?"

"No, I uh." He fumbled around for his next words. Maybe this was a mistake. *Abort! Abort!* "I mean, people are already talking about us. I thought what's the harm in us hanging out some time, you know?"

She rolled her eyes and began walking again. "That's not a good idea. I need to get to work."

Alex was ready to admit defeat. Then the piece of scratch paper in his hand caught his attention, reminding him he wasn't a quitter. He jogged up to Eva and shoved the paper into her hand. "My number in case you change your mind." He jogged back to the school to get ready for the game. He sensed her watching him go.

Alex was grateful for the distraction of the game that night. He could leave his troubles behind and get lost in the familiar rhythm of the game. But the minute they got back to the locker room, it all came rushing back. His stomach flipped with embarrassment. At least no one had witnessed Eva's complete and utter rejection of him.

He slammed his locker shut and someone patted him on the back. "Don't worry buddy, plenty of fish in the sea." Alex turned to see Collin towering over him, helmet still in hand.

"What?"

"I saw you and Eva talking. Ouch looked rough. But don't give up, bro. I've been working on dating Jai'Lune since the minute she moved here. I think I'm finally making progress though, you know? Your day will come too."

He'd been right at the lake. Collin *did* like Jai'Lune. Could he be getting this social cue stuff figured out? "Thanks, appreciate that." And he did. It was nice to have someone notice and say something. Collin was a good guy. He wished they were better friends.

As he left the school, there was a man walking down the sidewalk toward him. Alex mustered up a smile and a small wave so he wouldn't seem rude. The guy nodded his head to acknowledge Alex as he walked by. Something was off about the guy. It was enough to catch Alex's attention, even in his distracted state. The man's body was shimmering like light reflecting off a lake, and he was dressed like the old-fashioned farm hands in pictures from the 1930s. Alex's curiosity got the better of him, and he jogged back to the man. "Excuse me, sir."

The man didn't break his stride. "I'm going to visit my sister. I must see her before I can be movin' on."

What a weird answer. "I, uh, okay." Alex stopped walking and stood stunned at the weird response. Then he watched the man walk right through someone's closed front door. He blinked and rubbed his face. He needed to get some sleep.

Chapter Ten

By the time Eva got home, she was running late for work. She braced herself for another glare from Roxie as she clocked in and got busy setting tables for supper.

Her shift went by in a blur. She couldn't stop thinking about Alex asking if she wanted to hang out sometime. *She didn't want to, right?* He was trying to use her to make Janet jealous. It was the only explanation that made sense. Eva tried not to think about how nice he'd been at the lake.

On her way home, Eva grabbed the mail. She stood at the kitchen table and flipped through the stack, tossing the grocery store ads and other junk mail on the table. A pink envelope caught her attention. It had her name on it. She never got mail. She eyed the letter with a hint of excitement mixed with suspicion and the tiniest bit of unexplainable trepidation. The return address was somewhere in Marysburg. *What was this?*

Eva turned the envelope over in her hand and opened it. Inside was a white card with tiny pink flowers cascading down one side. A piece of notebook paper fell out and landed at her feet. She picked it up and read:

Eva, I know it's been a long time since we saw each other. A lifetime for you, actually. I'm sorry about that. I want to make it right.

Would you meet me for supper? How about this Friday? I'm making chili and cinnamon rolls. I know you are busy. I can wait if you need me to. God knows you've waited long enough for me to be the father you deserve. I'm sorry.

I love you, sweetheart, and pray for you every day. Let me know about Friday.

Dad

Dad. The word was awkward on the page, as if even the paper knew it was a lie. He'd never been her dad. More of a stranger. She was tempted to crumple the letter up and throw it away. Maybe light it on fire and watch it burn.

After all these years, she couldn't have supper with Russell and pretend everything was fine. Especially not with all the other things she was dealing with right now. Did he think he could abandon her for over a decade and waltz back into her life? Gramp's words echoed in her head. *Don't be building walls before you give him a chance.*

Eva cringed. Maybe she should meet with him once. After all, hadn't Gramps said her dad tried to come back for her? Maybe Mom was to blame for his absence. *Why had she shut him out of their lives?* Eva wasn't going to repeat her mistake. At least not until she had a good reason.

The local address and phone number were written across the bottom of the letter. Eva pulled out her phone, then hesitated. Should she call? Text? *What did one do when contacting their estranged father?* She couldn't trust her voice, so she texted. 'Friday works. See you at 6.' She pushed send fast before she could change her mind.

Eva's mom would freak out if she knew she was going to visit Russell. She needed a cover story in case her mom was around when she wanted to leave. Maybe she could tell her she was going to the football game to watch Jai'Lune play in the band. Mom would buy that. She'd probably be at work anyhow. Eva's phone buzzed with a text. 'Great, can't wait!'

Well, that was it then. Eva took a deep breath and let Flip in from the back yard. She walked to her room the way she did every other night of her life, but this night was different. This night, she had plans with her father.

Eva didn't dream about tornados that night. She dreamed about meeting Russell. It was a series of terrible events that unfolded one after another in her mind. She walked in and he'd forgotten she was coming. He heated up a frozen dinner and ate while watching football, ignoring her while she sat there devastated. By the time her alarm went off, she was exhausted and relieved to be put out of her restless misery. *Hey, at least she didn't have the tornado dreams.*

School was a welcome distraction, and Eva was glad when Jai'Lune said she could hang out that afternoon. They sat on her couch dunking cookies into their milk, and she pulled the letter from her father out of her pocket. She handed it to Jai'Lune and held her breath. Jai'Lune's eyes got bigger and bigger as she read the letter. "What are you going to do?"

"I'm going to see him Friday."

"No way!"

"Yep."

"Are you gonna tell your mom? I mean, does she know? Did she see the letter?"

"She doesn't know, and I'm going to keep it that way, at least for now. I'll go see him once to satisfy my curiosity. Then I'm done with him." *Probably.* "What's the point of telling Mom if it's not that big of a deal?"

"Not that big of a deal? Eva, you're meeting your *father* for the first time. It's an enormous deal."

"I know. Shut up, you're making me nervous!"

"I'm going with you," Jai'Lune said. It was a statement, not a question.

"You don't have to. I'll be fine!"

"I know you'll be fine, but this is not something you should do alone. I'll be there. Heck, I'll drive you. I'll pick you up at 5:45."

The lights flickered. "Ugh, why do the lights keep doing that?"

"I don't know," Jai'Lune said, but for a split second a look crossed her face and Eva had the weird thought maybe Jai'Lune knew something she wasn't saying. Eva shook her head, and the thought passed.

"What are you going to say when you meet him? I mean, after all this time, nothing will cut it," Jai'Lune pointed out.

"True. And in case you hadn't noticed, I'm not good at small talk."

She smirked. "Actually, I had noticed that."

"Ha, I bet. I figure, if he's the one inviting me, he better know what to say. I shouldn't have to worry about it, right?"

"You keep telling yourself that."

"I intend to," Eva said, pretending to be prim and proper. How did Jai'Lune always know how to lighten the mood, even when Eva told her the biggest news of her life? "I don't know what I'd ever do without you, Jai'Lune."

"Same, sister." Jai'Lune winked. "Here's hoping you never have to find out!"

Chapter Eleven

The next day, Eva sat through a science lecture, then Mrs. Meeks handed out worksheets announcing, "Work in partners or by yourself. It's your choice." *Oh, Mrs. Meeks, my fellow introvert.* Another reason to love her.

Eva worked alone and finished before everyone else. She grabbed the giant wooden key that served as the restroom pass and headed to the bathroom. Grace was washing her hands when Eva walked in. Grace's voice sounded weak when she said hello. The whites of her eyes were red as she glanced at Eva in the mirror.

When Eva came out of the stall, Grace was still there, splashing water on her face. She patted her cheeks dry with one of the coarse brown paper towels. Some stray droplets landed on Eva's arm. "Oh, sorry. Did I splash you?"

"Don't worry about it. Why won't these stupid things ever turn on?" Eva asked, waving her hand in front of the faucet sensor. "It's like I have to prove my existence to get some water." Grace chuckled a little as she reached over and waved her hand once. The water poured out.

"I guess you're alive. Thanks," Eva said.

Grace shrugged. “Doesn’t feel like it.”

“You okay?” Eva couldn’t help but ask.

“Not really. I’m still having those dreams, Eva. They won’t stop. They’re driving me nuts.”

“Did you talk to your grandma about them this weekend?”

“Great grandma. And no, the rug rats were running around like maniacs, and there wasn’t ever a good time. I’m going over there after cheerleading practice tonight to talk to her.”

“That’ll be good. Can you let me know if you figure out anything?”

“Sure, you better give me your phone number. I don’t think I have it.” They swapped numbers and Eva headed back to class, a little less alone in the whole dream saga.

Jai'Lune caught Eva at her locker. “What are you doing after school?”

“I think I’m gonna take a nap.”

She scrunched up her nose as if to say, *what’s wrong with you?*

“I’m tired. I don’t know. Maybe I’m coming down with something.”

“Okay, well, I hope you get better soon. Can you call me later?”

“Sure. What’s up?”

“I need to tell you something.”

“Well, now you’ve got me curious. Let’s go to my house and hang out.”

“Okay,” she said with a smile. She was such an expert at getting Eva to do what she wanted. By the time they got to Eva’s house, she wasn’t tired. Being with Jai'Lune always made everything better. She let Flip in, and the dog earned her name, flipping out with excitement when she saw Jai'Lune. She jumped up and down, spun around in circles and settled into sniffing both.

"That dog has always loved you," Eva said.

"What can I say? I'm lovable." Jai'Lune laughed. Flip nuzzled her hand in classic *pet me* dog language, and Jai'Lune humored her. "Who's a good dog?"

Eva poured two glasses of milk, and they settled on the couch with a package of cookies. She tossed a blanket at Jai'Lune, and they both nestled in, even though the air outside still hadn't turned cold.

"What's up?" Eva asked.

"Lots of stuff," she said with a conspiratorial grin.

Eva rolled her eyes, but Jai'Lune ignored her and went on. "People are saying Alex asked you out, and you blew him off."

Was nothing private anymore? Of course, it wasn't... not in a small town.

"Yeah, so?" Eva said, shrugging her shoulders.

Jai'Lune gasped. "Is it true? People asked me, and I said, 'No way, she would have told me.' Why didn't you tell me, you jerk?" She bopped Eva's arm.

"I don't know. I guess I forgot."

"Forgot? The hottest guy in school asks you out and you . . . forget? Oh no biggie, this stuff happens to me all the time?"

"No," Eva said, to defend herself. "He asked me after school the other day, and I had to go straight to work. By the time I got off, I guess it slipped my mind. I have something I've kind of been struggling with that I need to talk to you about." Finally, she told Jai'Lune about the dreams and all the strange things that had been happening lately.

"And you're just *now* telling me this?"

"Well, at first, I thought the dreams were no big deal. Then they got worse, and I was going to tell you on the way to the lake, but Vanessa was there. And, I don't know, it was like if I talked about them too much, they'd be more real. But now it's all too much. I had to tell you."

"Of course, you had to tell me! I'm your best friend, Eva. My job is to help you when you're going through stuff like this. I got you, girl." She leaned over and hugged Eva.

"Thanks. I know."

"And Grace is having the same dreams?"

"Yup."

Jai'Lune shivered. "That's messed up."

"Tell me about it."

Jai'Lune left around suppertime, and Eva was doing her homework when her phone rang. It was a weird number, probably spam. No one else ever called her except Gramps and Gram. At the last second, her curiosity made her answer. "Hello?"

"Eva?"

"Yeah."

"This is Grace. I talked to my Great Granny. Can you meet me at the church tonight?"

"The church?" Eva was confused.

"I can't think of any other place we can be alone, and I need to talk to you in private. Plus, if I tell my parents I'm going to church, they won't pummel me with questions."

Eva glanced at the clock. It was almost seven. "Sure, what time?"

"How about in a few minutes? I'm going there now."

"Okay, which church?" Their small town had *three* churches.

"The Catholic one." There was only one Catholic church. It's where her grandparents and half the town went. Eva rolled her eyes at the thought of meeting there. Would she burst into unholy flames the minute she walked through the door? She wasn't Catholic and hadn't been to any church in years.

When she was little and her mom was at work, she spent the weekends with Gram and Gramps. On Sunday, she'd end up going to the Catholic church with them. But her mom never made her go, and she hadn't been there for years, ever since she was old enough to stay home by herself all weekend. But it wasn't as though there were a lot of other places to meet in town if they wanted privacy, and she wanted to know what Grace was all worked up about.

"Okay, see you soon," Eva said. She threw some butter, bologna, and cheese on a couple slices of bread, let Flip out, and turned to leave. She almost collided with her mom at the door. "Whoa, honey, where you off to?"

"Meeting up with a friend. We're working on a project together."

Her mom gave Eva a tired smile. "Okay, don't stay out too late."

"I won't."

The church was only five blocks from Eva's house, but she had no desire to ride her bike in the dark tonight. She opted for Rusty, the name she'd affectionately given the rusty hand-me-down vehicle Gramps scrounged up for her on her sixteenth birthday. When she pulled up, Grace's small, silver car was already in the parking lot. Eva shoved the last bite of sandwich in her mouth and hopped out.

Eva was glad she wasn't the first one there. The last thing she wanted was to sit in an empty church alone—creepy! Maybe Grace felt the same because she was sitting in her car waiting for Eva. She jogged over. "Hey."

"Hey," Eva said. The scene was a little bleak, and she wondered what Grace had found out from her grandma. Grace pushed open the huge wooden church doors and Eva had a flashback to one of her dreams. She shook her head and stepped inside.

Grace dipped her finger in one of the small bowls of water attached to the wall on either side of the doors. She touched her forehead, belly button, left shoulder, then right. Eva walked past the water, not sure if she should follow suit and do the same with the water or if she wasn't allowed to, since she wasn't Catholic. The Catholic faith had always been a mystery to her—some secret society her mom didn't want her to be part of.

Grace knelt on one knee, rose again, and walked into a pew in the back of the church. Eva sat down beside her, and Grace turned to face her. "How's it going?" she asked, as if she needed to work up to the important stuff.

"I'm okay. Tired. How about you?" Eva was trying to hold back her impatience with a smile.

"I'm alright. I talked to Great Granny. She's sworn to secrecy, and I know I can trust her."

"Okay, what'd she say?" *Spit it out already.*

"Well, I guess way back, when our parents were in school, some kids were having the same dreams we are."

Eva's skin crawled a bit at the thought of this going back any further than a few months. She tried to stay calm, though. "Okay."

"Eva, this might be hard to hear, but Great Granny said your parents were having the dreams."

"What?"

"They were the talk of the town back then. It was real messed up what happened to them. I guess their dreams only had two tornados, not three. Your parents were trying to figure out what the dreams meant, and the town got pretty shook up about it. Your mom got pregnant with you and everything kinda fell apart."

"What do you mean, fell apart?"

"Well, your dad got sent to live with his own dad, and no one was trying to figure it out anymore. But Great Granny said the dreams made her curious, so she's done some research over the years. Not internet research—she doesn't even have a computer—but town records and religious books." Grace put her hands on her knees and leaned toward Eva.

"This is where it gets weird." *Maybe for her.* This was already weird for Eva. "Have you ever thought the tornados were going to cut open the sky and pour darkness out on everyone?"

Eva nodded.

"Me too. According to Great Granny, these dreams have been happening to teenagers in this town since it was first settled over one hundred years ago. The first people who had the dreams stirred things up. It divided the town. Half the town thought they were crazy or evil. The other half thought everyone should listen to the kids."

"That's why the town is divided. Have you ever noticed that? All the super old houses are on the way north and the way south side of town. The closer you get to the middle, the newer the houses are. Every other small town around here is the opposite. The old houses are at the center and the town grew around it."

Eva nodded. She had noticed that. It's one of the few things she loved about Marysburg. Because of the layout and flat ground, she could stand in the center of town and still see corn fields on all four sides.

Grace went on. "The people who believed the kids settled on one side. The people who didn't believe them settled on the opposite side." Grace took a deep breath. "Granny thinks the dreams are a warning. All those years ago, their dreams only had one tornado. By the time your parents were having the dreams, there were two tornados. Now ours have three. Great Granny says three is a number of completion."

Goosebumps formed on Eva's arms. She knew what Grace was going to say next, if what she'd learned was anything like what Eva had read on the internet. "Great Granny thinks, whatever it is, it's coming soon."

"Does she have any idea what *it* might be?" Eva asked, with more hope in her voice than she wanted.

"Kind of. You know how Catholics believe there's a spiritual world in battle?"

Nope. She gave Grace a blank stare.

"Well, there're these angels who used to be with God, but Lucifer wanted to be like God, so he took a stand. All these other angels followed him and there was a battle. Lucifer and the angels who followed him were thrown down to Earth. Now Lucifer is the devil, and all the other fallen angels are demons who prowl about the world, seeking the ruin of souls. The battle is still going on. That's why we pray for protection every week at the end of Mass."

"You do?" Eva didn't remember any of that from her few visits to the Catholic church.

Grace nodded. "The good angels are trying to protect humans and the evil angels are trying to destroy us. Granny thinks the evil is ramping up big time."

"Ramping up how?" Eva asked.

"She's worried the battle is getting worse. Much worse. The angels are trying to hold off the demons, but Granny's worried that the angels won't be able to hold the evil off much longer. Soon it will pour into our world. It's what we sense as the true threat in our dreams. Our dreams are the warning."

Eva shuddered and rubbed her goosebumps. "Great Granny says we need to pray God gives the angels strength and maybe the darkness won't pour into our world. She's hoping it's not too late."

Someone stood at the front of the church, making Grace and Eva jump. They hadn't realized anyone else was there. Eva was glad they had been whispering. Hopefully, the person didn't hear what they said. They sat in silence as the person trudged down the aisle toward them. The sun was setting, and suddenly she realized how dark the church was.

As the person got closer, Eva could tell it was a guy. Not just any guy. It was Alex. He was walking with his head down, lost in his own world.

Chapter Twelve

The dim light of the empty church always comforted Alex when he had a lot on his mind. There was no one there to impress. No one expected anything from him. It was the perfect place to sit, rest, and clear his head.

He wondered if life would be easier if he could talk to someone about the dreams and that crazy attack. Who would he even tell, though? Not any of the guys on his team, that's for sure. Not his parents. They'd think he was crazy. And Pops —maybe he'd understand. But Alex couldn't work up the nerve to tell him when they were fishing last weekend. He didn't want the one person he could be himself around to wonder if he was losing his mind.

Life would be easier if he could make a good friend. Most guys didn't want to talk about their feelings or dreams, though. Everyone he knew wanted to throw the football around and brag about their latest conquest. It'd be okay. The dreams couldn't go on forever, right? Seasons change. Problems move on. It was only a phase. *Maybe a growth spurt?*

Alex took a deep breath, stood up, and left the pew. He

knelt and made the sign of the cross, then turned toward the back of the church. Someone else was there. Geez, he'd been so lost in thought he didn't even hear them come in.

As he got closer to the back of the church, Alex realized it was Eva and Grace. He stifled a groan. His pride was still hurting from how thoroughly she had rejected him. The last thing he wanted was to see her here in the one place where he could escape his problems. "Hey," he said with a little wave in their direction, hoping to slip out with no more embarrassing conversations.

"Hi," Grace and Eva said in unison.

"How are you, Alex?" Grace asked, her eyebrows knit together. "Doing okay? Tough practice tonight?" Of course, Grace wouldn't let him go without making him talk. Ever since they were little, Grace was always poking her nose in other people's business, trying to mother everyone.

"Practice was fine. I just haven't been getting the best sleep."

"Oh?" Grace's voice sounded tight. It made Alex look at her. "Bad dreams?"

How did she know? Maybe she was joking. Alex squinted, trying to decide. *What the heck, he'd play along.* If she was joking, he could pretend he was, too. "Yep, you know. Same old, same old. Black tornados threatening to kill everyone."

Grace and Eva both went still and stared at him. "What?" He asked, his face flush.

"Alex, we're having the same dreams," Grace said in a low voice.

Alex's eyes shot from Grace's face to Eva's. He didn't think they were messing with him. Why would they? But they couldn't be serious.

Grace nodded, her ponytail bobbing. "We figured it out at the lake. Eva found some people online that are having them too. My Great Granny says they're a warning."

Alex folded his arms across his chest. "What kind of warning?"

Grace leaned forward and told him what her Great Granny said about the history of the dreams in their town and what she thought the dreams meant. When she was done, he didn't know what to say so, for once, he said what he was thinking, "Sounds creepy."

"I know. It's totally creepy. And if it's true, we don't have much time before whatever is going to happen...happens. Granny said we need to pray hard."

"We pray the St. Michael prayer every week at the end of Mass. Isn't that enough?"

Grace shrugged.

"The St. Michael prayer?" Eva asked.

Alex had forgotten she wasn't Catholic. "St. Michael the Archangel, defend us in battle. Be our defense against the wickedness and snares of the devil. May God rebuke him, we humbly pray, and do thou, O Prince of the heavenly hosts, by the power of God, thrust into hell Satan, and all the evil spirits, who prowl about the world seeking the ruin of souls. Amen."

He said the prayer without thinking as he always did in Mass. Alex never considered it might mean something, let alone ever ponder what the meaning was.

"Crazy," Eva said, and he wondered what she meant by that. The dim lights in the church flickered off for the briefest moment and back on. "Ugh, here too?" Eva said.

"What do you mean?" Grace asked.

"My lights keep doing that at home. Flickering on and off randomly. Lightbulbs burning out. It's creepy."

"Mine too," Grace said to Eva with a nod. Alex realized his lights had been doing the same thing, but he hadn't given it much thought. Their old farmhouse always had quirks. He had to admit it was weird though, if it was happening to all three of them.

"I think we should say the St. Michael prayer every night before bed. At least until we figure out what else to do. It can't hurt, right?" Grace said.

"I don't know the prayer," Eva pointed out.

"Father always has extra prayer cards in the back. Let me find you one." Alex walked to the back counter of the church to search for a prayer card while Eva and Grace whispered in their pew.

On Sundays, when his parents talked forever, Alex fended off the boredom by checking out all the random stuff Father put out on the back counter. Some of it was interesting. He knew he'd seen a card with the St. Michael prayer somewhere a few weeks back. It took him a bit to sift through everything, but he found it. The card had a painting of Jesus with streams of blue and red coming from his body on one side and the St. Michael prayer on the other.

The girls walked up, and Alex handed the card to Eva. "Here, you can keep it. They're free," he said, feeling dumb. *Of course they're free, you idiot.*

"Thanks," she said with a crooked smile. The way she held the card reminded him of how she held the beer at the lake, as if she wasn't quite sure what to do with it.

"Okay, talk soon," Grace said, and they all walked toward the door. As they did, Alex had a strange sensation of déjà vu. He'd been in this church with these two in his dreams before, the tornados howling outside those big wooden doors. Alex turned to the pews, almost expecting to see people from their town annoyed as they stared back at him. But the pews were empty. In that moment, he realized how utterly exhausted he was. Maybe he'd sleep well tonight.

At least now he wasn't alone. Someone else knew about the dreams. Not only that, but they were *having* them too. He never would have guessed his day would turn out this way. On his drive home, Alex wondered if the prayer would make any difference. At least it was something to try. Why hadn't he thought of it before? Because prayer was a last resort. The thing he did when nothing else worked. He felt bad about it, but it was true.

Chapter Thirteen

Eva was about to doze off when she remembered the prayer card Alex gave her at church. A twinge of guilt poked her to get up and find it. She never prayed, but she had promised Alex and Grace she would. And what if it could help? She'd try about anything if it would help. She hopped out of bed, dug the card out of her jeans pocket and snuggled under the warm covers on her bed again. Using her phone as a flashlight, she read the words out loud.

"St. Michael the Archangel, defend us in battle. Be our defense against the wickedness and snares of the devil. May God rebuke him, we humbly pray, and do thou, O Prince of the heavenly hosts, by the power of God, thrust into hell Satan, and all the evil spirits, who prowl about the world seeking the ruin of souls. Amen."

The prayer could use some editing. It didn't flow well, and when she was done, nothing happened. What did she expect? Fireworks? A voice from heaven? No. That's not how it worked. Eva laid the prayer card on her nightstand and turned off her phone.

She let her thoughts drift to what Grace said about her

parents and there being a long history of people having the dreams in Marysburg. Did that mean something? Could Marysburg somehow be an epicenter of evil? Eva shook her head. Nothing significant ever happened in Marysburg, and nothing ever would.

~

The only thing that could get Eva out of bed the next day was the thought of Ellie's donuts. When she pushed the glass café door open, a bell dinged. Ellie glanced up from behind the counter and wiped her hands on the flowery apron she was wearing over jeans and a faded red t-shirt.

You could always count on Ellie to be consistent. She was about Gramps and Gram's age. Her hair, which had been somewhere between blonde and gray Eva's whole life, was cut short in a no-nonsense style that matched her personality. It was the same every day. *Did she wake up that way?* Eva wouldn't survive such a lack of change in her own life, but this morning she appreciated the steadiness Ellie provided.

"You look like death warmed over, child. You okay?" Ellie always got straight to the point.

"Hi, Ellie. I'm okay. Haven't been sleeping the best."

"Well, you take care a yourself. You hear? There're two things I always say we oughta do, and I've lived by them my whole life. Ain't had a cold in ten years. Praise the Lord. All you gotta do is drink lots a water and get plenty a rest." Ellie raised her gargantuan jug of ice water off the counter.

"Makes sense." She knew not to argue with Ellie.

"Now that's a good girl. Grab one a those bottles a water. It's on the house."

"Thanks, Ellie." Eva grabbed a water, along with two glazed donuts. It was nice to have someone to talk to in the mornings. When she left for school, her mom was usually at work or sleeping.

Eva paid for her donuts, smiled at Ellie, and stepped out into the gentle morning sunshine. A breeze stirred the wisps of hair around her face, and she took a deep breath of the fragrant morning air. Crisp, fall mornings always held so much possibility. Anything could happen, and if it did, it just might change your life.

Eva had managed to ignore the fact that she was meeting Russell all week thanks to the distractions of the dreams and meeting with Grace and Alex. But on Thursday, she decided to cancel with Russell. Why should she meet him anyhow? What good would it do? The lights in her room flickered as she pulled her phone out to text him. Gramps' words popped into her head, nudging her conscience. *I don't want you going and getting poisoned to him on accountta what other people think. You make up your own mind about him, you hear?*

Okay, okay. She'd go. Once.

All day Friday, her stomach was in knots. She was glad Mom wasn't home after school. She'd bought Eva's lie about the football game, but if she noticed Eva acting weird, she'd know something was up. The next two hours were an eternity, but at 5:45 sharp, Jai'Lune pulled up in her driveway.

After a quick hello, they drove the short distance to Russell's house in silence. Jai'Lune must have sensed the quiet was what Eva needed. Before she knew it, they were standing on the front porch of an old farmhouse. Eva lifted her arm to knock, but let it drop without knocking.

"What are you doing? You have to actually tap on the door."

"I can't do this."

"Yes, you can. You are strong and I'm right here with you. It's going to be fine. And remember, you only have to see him this one time."

"Just once."

"Ready?" Eva nodded and Jai'Lune knocked on the door with four confident taps.

Panic flooded through Eva's body and her thoughts raced. *What should she do? What would she say? Oh, hey, how's life? How's it going, stranger? What've you been up to?* Every question was loaded with the abandonment of a lifetime. Her throat was getting tight, and she touched the inhaler in her coat pocket for comfort. It was there. Just in case.

The door swung open, and Eva stood face-to-face with her father for the first time in her life. They stared at each other for an eternity and the blink of an eye.

Eva took in every detail of the quiet, almost shy man in front of her. She'd expected a skinny drunk with greasy, scraggly hair. This man was not at all what she'd expected. He wore a cardigan and jeans. His hair was short but looked like it could use a trim, and his intense, dark brown eyes—the same eyes she saw in the mirror every morning—stared back at her with an uncanny wisdom that surprised her.

An old memory came rushing at her, and Eva took a step back, the force of the memory almost knocking her down. She was young, maybe five or six, and she was swinging at the tiny park in town. Mom was sitting at a picnic table across the park when a strange man came up to her mom. A man who was strikingly similar to the one standing in front of her.

The man and her mom argued. Then he left. Eva watched him walk across the grass to his car. As he opened the door, he turned and peered at her for a long moment. Her gaze was drawn to his, and she stared back, powerless to look away. He got in his car and drove away.

Eva ran over to her mom and asked who the man was. Her

mom had tears in her eyes but had a harsh tone to her voice. "Nobody important. Go play." Eva knew better than to ask more. After that day, she heard her mom crying herself to sleep every night for a month. But neither one of them had ever mentioned the man again.

Eva never put two and two together until this moment. *Could it have been him?* Had he been trying to see her all those years ago? The ache of it almost brought Eva to her knees.

"Hello, Eva," the man finally said with an awkward, slanted smile. He stepped through the door, joining Eva and Jai'Lune on the front porch, and gestured toward a group of worn, white wicker chairs. "Would you like to sit? The chili is ready, and I just put the cinnamon rolls in the oven. Can I get you some water or iced tea?" His words were rushed, and she realized he was nervous, too.

Eva nodded. "Water. Please."

"Nothing for me, thanks." Eva glanced at Jai'Lune. She'd almost forgotten she was there. Jai'Lune gave her a smile that said *it'll be fine.*

Eva nodded in response to the unspoken words and took a seat. Russell stepped back into the house and she forced herself to take slow, deep breaths.

"That went well." Jai'Lune smirked with sarcasm. "Need your inhaler?"

"I'm fine." *For now.* Eva was glad to have a few minutes to catch her breath before Russell came back to the porch. She gazed around at the old farm place. Despite its age, it was well kept. It had a long lane that cut a grove of trees in half. She could see the road stretching out beyond and corn fields brown and drying up for the harvest. Two of the trees were bending over as if to hug each other, and their embrace held her gaze. This porch was the kind of place you could sit forever. It was comforting and calm.

What a strange contrast to the storm of emotions brewing

inside Eva. The screen door slammed shut, snapping her out of her thoughts. She watched Russell walk across the porch. He handed her a glass of ice water with a smile and sat in the wicker chair across from her. "Eva, I'm glad you're here."

"Thanks."

Eva had no clue what to say next. All her unanswered questions swirled in her mind, but she couldn't trust herself to speak. She wanted to get right to it. Ask him why he left and why he was back. But that might be a little too much all at once, even for her. "I'm not sure what to call you," she finally blurted, twisting her glass in her hands, grateful to have something to hold on to.

Russell paused before answering. "How about 'Russell' for now?" Eva nodded and stared at her lap. "How's school going for you two? You're a senior, right?"

Eva nodded. Jai'Lune was sitting comfortably in her chair as if this was her house and he was the guest. Eva wondered how she could be relaxed in such an intense moment. "I'm a senior too. Go cats." Jai'Lune pumped her fist in the air with a healthy dose of sarcastic school spirit.

Eva was grateful for these easy questions. It reminded her of a test. First question, what is your name? She almost always got that one right. But now Russell had a look of uncertainty. Maybe he was struggling for his next words too?

In that moment, Eva realized if she was only ever going to see Russell once in her whole life, she better make every moment count. "What brought you back to town?" Ellie wasn't the only one who could get straight to the point.

"Well, it's... complicated," he said, pausing. "Truth be told, you're the reason I'm back, Eva. I'm sorry I haven't been there for you in the past."

That took the wind out of her lungs, and she wrapped her fingers around the inhaler in her pocket. With her other hand, she gripped her glass, the only anchor keeping her from losing it. Struggling to hold back tears, she watched a drop of condensation slide down her glass as if it were crying for her.

"Why now? After all these years, why come back now?" Eva held her breath.

"Well, Eva, that's where things get complicated." He glanced at Jai'Lune and said, "Let's go inside first. I need to check on the cinnamon rolls and we can talk in there."

Chapter Fourteen

Eva let out a breath and urged her lungs to pull in more air as she stepped through the door into Russell's living room. It was a small, cozy space and the smell of chili and cinnamon rolls was homey. A TV sat across from the front door with a fireplace underneath. A faded couch was facing it with an old knit blanket draped over the back of it.

"That's my mom's blanket," Eva said without thinking. *What a stupid thing to say.* But she couldn't help it. It was the exact same blanket that had been on her mom's bed for as long as she could remember.

"Your grandma knit Rachel and me matching blankets for Christmas one year," he said with a smile. It was strange to hear him say her mom's name in such a familiar tone. To think this stranger knew her grandparents. But of course, he did. Gramps had told her about it.

A book with a black leather cover lay open on the coffee table with a highlighter resting in the binding. It was similar to the Bible Eva read to Nora that night at the nursing home. The room was growing darker by the moment as the sun set, and Russell flipped on a light. The lightbulb popped and went black.

"Why does that keep happening? Something weird is going on with the lights in this town," Eva said. Jai'Lune and Russell exchanged glances and shrugged.

"Hard to say in this old house. About everything needs fixing. The kitchen's over here." Russell gestured to the right.

The kitchen was tucked into a nook that jutted out toward the side of the house. It was outdated with old metal cabinets. The table and chairs reminded her of the ones at Ellie's Cafe. Eva paused in the doorway. Jai'Lune draped her arm over Eva's shoulders. "It's going to be okay, Eva."

She gave Jai'Lune a *How do you know?* glance then turned her attention to Russell. He was fussing around the kitchen, stirring the chili, peeking at the cinnamon rolls in the oven and filling water glasses. "Okay, a little longer on the rolls. We can chat in the living room." He led the way and sat down on an overstuffed chair. Eva perched on the edge of the couch and Jai'Lune sat down beside her.

Russell's hands pressed together in front of him. "I think you might be the kind of person who prefers to get straight to the point."

"Pretty much." *At least in this situation.*

He took a deep breath. "Well, there's no easy way to say this, so I guess I'll get to it. When I was in high school, some strange things happened to me. I had these dreams with a couple tornados in them."

Eva sucked in a breath. *Grace's Granny was right.* He glanced up with a question in his eyes before continuing. "Your mom began having the same dreams. We found out some other kids in town, Charlie Smith and Spencer O'Donnell, were having them, too."

Eva's eyes got wide. Spencer O'Donnell was Grace's dad.

That was an interesting detail Grace's Granny—or Grace—had omitted. She tried to hide her surprise.

Russell went on, "We didn't know what the dreams meant, and they were driving us nuts. We tried to talk to some adults about it. They told us to be quiet, ignore them, and they'd go away. Every time we brought it up, the adults got more and more upset."

"Why'd they get upset?"

"People fear what they don't understand. But we couldn't ignore the dreams, and they didn't go away. In fact, they escalated. We started seeing things when we were awake too. Some people said we were possessed by the devil. Others said we were on drugs. But we weren't." He squinted at Eva as if checking for understanding and she nodded.

Russell stood and leaned his arm on the mantel, staring into the spot where the fire was only a memory. "The other kids having the dreams got scared. They wanted it all to stop so they could go back to normal, whatever normal is. One by one, they figured out how to ignore the dreams until they went away. It all stopped for them, and your mom and I were the only two still having the dreams. Still trying to figure out what they meant."

The timer went off, interrupting Russell's story. "Oh," he said, distracted. "Okay, let's eat." Eva wasn't hungry, but she and Jai'Lune followed Russell into the kitchen. He pulled the cinnamon rolls out of the oven and moved the chili to the table. He dished up soup for all of them and sat down. "Are you okay if we pray?"

Eva shrugged. He folded his hands and bowed his head. She glanced at Jai'Lune and did the same. He said the prayer they always prayed at Gramps and Gram's house. Eva had it memorized from childhood, and she mumbled along with him. When they had finished, she took a bite of the cinnamon roll, and it melted in her mouth. It was delicious.

Between bites, Russell continued telling his story as if he sensed this was his one shot with her and he didn't want to waste it. "Your mom and I couldn't let it drop. We had a sense there was a message we were meant to carry—something bigger than us that was going on. I was driving my mom nuts trying to figure it all out. She told me I was going to ruin my life and hers if I didn't shut up about the whole thing. That's right about when your mom got pregnant with you."

"It was the final straw for my mom. She shipped me off to live with my dad. He was a real drunk. I was isolated at his house. I didn't know anyone, and I was missing your mom like crazy. My dad always had beer in the fridge. One night I grabbed one, then another, and I didn't stop—not that night and not the next."

"My dad didn't have two pennies to rub together. He spent everything on booze. There was no way to get down to see your mom." Russell's hands played with his cinnamon roll, but he didn't take a bite. "One day, your mom showed up on my doorstep and surprised me. Course I was drunk as a sailor when she got there. She turned right back around and headed home. Said I'd never see her or our baby again. Said she didn't need a drunk in her life and we were through."

"I don't blame her. She was trying to watch out for you, even though she was just a kid herself. We were under some powerful spiritual attacks by then, and the evil was trying to divide and conquer Rachel and me. Course, I didn't understand all that yet, and I sure as heck wasn't strong enough to fight back."

"Attacks?"

"Well, this is where it gets mighty hard to grasp. I'm talking about the evil, Eva. The darkness."

Eva leaned back in her chair and her muscles tensed. Was he crazy? She glanced at the door. It was too far away for her and Jai'Lune to escape before he could catch them. But he couldn't catch both at the same time. Maybe one could get away and call for help.

She remembered what Grace's Granny had said about the dreams being a warning. Was this more of the same? Were they both crazy or neither?

Russell must have sensed Eva's reaction, because he raised his eyebrows. "I'm sorry, Eva. I didn't mean to scare you. I know people don't usually talk about this kind of stuff. We're blinded by the visible world and forget there's an invisible world all around us. Maybe it was too soon to spring this on you. I just have this sense we don't have much time. I have something for you." *Was he trying to change the subject?*

He stood up and went to a wooden cupboard in the dining room rifling through drawers. Maybe they should take this opportunity to leave. Eva raised her eyebrows and tilted her head toward the door, but Jai'Lune shook her head as if saying *no, it'll be fine.* The lights flickered and out of the corner of her eye, Eva saw a young woman in an old-fashioned dress standing with her hands on her hips watching Russell. Eva turned her head to get a better look at the woman, but she was gone.

Russell came back holding a necklace out to Eva. "This is a crucifix—a cross with Jesus on it. It was your great-great-great-grandmother Lucy's. She was a powerful prayer warrior. The necklace is a blessed object. When you wear it, it's a sign to the darkness you are protected by God."

The cross glinted in the light as Eva held out her hand to accept the gift and Russell laid it in her hand. The silver was cool in her warm palm. The idea of having something from her, however-many-greats grandmother, was intriguing. The details on the cross were worn smooth, and you could tell it was old. She opened the necklace clasp and reached around, clicking it securely into place at the back of her neck. She smiled at the spot in the room where she'd seen the woman and a warm peace emanated through her heart.

Eva turned to Russell. "Thanks. We better get going." She needed time to process. This was all... a lot.

"I understand," he said to the air as Jai'Lune and Eva stepped out into the dark.

As they walked to the car, Eva heard the dead leaves crunch under her feet and the smell of change drifted up from the ground. She slammed the car door shut and rested her forehead on the dash. The cold plastic did nothing to calm her. Eva's mind was racing. She needed wide-open space. Where could she go?

"Would you mind dropping me at my grandparent's house?" she asked Jai'Lune.

"Sure. Why?"

"I don't want to risk bumping into Mom right now. I need some time to be alone."

"I get that," Jai'Lune said. "Do you want to talk about it? I mean, that was some crazy stuff. It might help to talk it out."

"Eventually, but not right now. I need to let it sink in, you know? It's almost too much for my brain to comprehend at the moment."

"Okay," Jai'Lune said. "Call or text if you need anything. A ride home, someone to process with. I'm here for you. I can come back, keep you company. Whatever you need."

"I know," Eva said, and tried to give Jai'Lune a reassuring smile.

As they pulled into the drive, Eva could see the creek cutting through the pasture north of Gram's and Gramp's house. She hopped out of the car, waited until Jai'Lune left, then made her way toward the creek. She needed quiet, water, and nature. She'd love to saddle up one of the horses and go riding, but she didn't have time for that. The tears were welling up behind her eyes. Any minute, she was going to lose it.

The full moon was a streetlight as she picked her way down the muddy bank of the creek. Large rocks served as steppingstones. Eva carefully balanced on each one as she walked across the creek. Then she followed the gentle bends in the creek until she came to a gigantic branch from an old oak tree that lay across the creek. The pale, vulnerable bark where the branch had once connected to the tree trunk was now exposed and shone bright in the moonlight.

The huge branch was inviting her to come sit. She pushed on it to test its strength, and it was sturdy. Eva put her hands on the rough bark and lifted herself up. The branch still had a few leaves desperately clinging to the life they once knew. She could relate.

She sat with her feet dangling over one side of the branch, the water dancing in the moonlight beneath her. Here, wrapped in the safety of solitude, she let the tears flow. Big fat alligator tears traced their way down Eva's cheeks, accentuated by sobs that ripped from her throat. It was an ugly cry as all the pain of a lifetime without her father came flowing out of her, echoing the water bubbling over the rocks below.

Finally, she cried herself out. The sobs faded, and the tears dried up as the peace of this place soothed her. She loved the wide-open space and being able to see whatever was coming at her from miles away.

The sound of movement made her jump. She whipped her head around in the darkness. "Who's there?"

Chapter Fifteen

Alex was helping Pops with chores when they heard something or someone wailing down by the stream. "What in the world? Is that a sick cow?" Pops asked.

Alex paused, listening. "I'm not sure. I'll go check it out."

"Take the shotgun."

Alex nodded and jogged to the barn. He grabbed the shotgun where it rested in the corner and headed toward the creek. He followed the sound, and it grew louder as he drew closer, then it went silent. There was a branch that fell over the creek in a storm a few months ago, and a shadow was on top of it. Alex squinted as he slowed his steps and drew nearer. Was it a mountain lion? They'd seen more and more of those in the area, but a mountain lion didn't make the sounds they'd heard.

As he drew closer, he stepped on a stick, and it made a loud crack in the dark. "Who's there?" the shadow figure asked.

He couldn't believe what he was seeing. "Eva?"

"Who is it?" she asked, sounding vulnerable in the moonlight.

"It's me. It's Alex," he said, holding up his hands in surrender.

"Alex? What are you doing out here?"

"I was helping Pops with chores, and we heard something. Thought maybe it was a sick cow. I told him I'd check it out."

She blushed in the moonlight. "Gee, thanks."

"I didn't mean that," he tried to backpedal. *Nice one, Alex. Every girl loves to be compared to a sick cow.* "I just, what I meant to say is, are you alright?" Alex climbed up on the branch beside her.

"I'm fine." She sighed. "Actually, I'm not fine at all. I met my father tonight."

"Really?" He didn't know much about her dad other than he left before she was born. Kids said some mean things, but he doubted any of it was true. He didn't know what to say next, so he kept it simple. "How'd it go?"

She was silent for a moment, and he wondered if he'd said the wrong thing. She spoke, sounding small in the dark. "Okay, I guess." At first, he didn't think she would elaborate, but after a long pause, she went on. "He said some weird stuff, Alex. Kind of what Grace's Great Granny said. And supposedly he and my mom had the dreams too when they were younger." She stared at Alex with wide, red-rimmed eyes. "What do you think? Is any of it true? And if it is, what'd we get ourselves into?"

"Honestly, I don't know."

"Me either." They sat in comfortable silence for several moments. There was something different about being with Eva compared to Janet. With Janet, there was no silence. Only talking and opinions, gossip, and drama. If he never had to deal with another day of drama his whole life, he would be glad. But the dreams and attacks were bringing their own kind of ominous drama.

Eva was saying something, and he tried to focus on her

words. "Do you ever wonder why *you*? I mean, why us? Grace's parents had the dreams too you know. She left that part out though when she told me what she knew... or maybe her Granny did."

Alex wasn't sure what to make of that. It was significant that both Grace's parents and Eva's had the dreams. "Maybe it's some kind of crazy spiritual heritage or something." *Did his parents have the dreams too?* No. They would have said something, right?

"I hadn't thought of it that way, but you're right." Eva gazed at him in the moonlight with a glint of what appeared to be respect. "You're not at all what I thought you were."

"Is that good?"

"Maybe."

"How did you think I'd be?"

"Like all the other guys."

Alex laughed. "And what are all the other guys like?"

"Shallow. Condescending. Boring. Self-interested. Basic."

"Geez, ouch."

"Sorry. I don't mean to be harsh." She turned to him. "You just... have a depth to you I wasn't expecting."

"Thanks." *She got all of that from sitting on a log with him?* But it sounded like a good thing, so he'd take it. "Does this mean you changed your mind about the date?"

"Don't push your luck." She smirked.

Alex smiled back, a spark of hope flickering in his heart that hadn't been there before. "You wanna go for a walk?" he asked.

"Walk? Now?"

"Sure, why not? It's something to do." He never could sit still for long.

"Uh, I guess," she said.

It wasn't a first date, but it was a start. At least she said yes to *something*. "Do you know what's over that hill?" Alex pointed. "It's on our property, but ever since I was little Pops made me promise not to wander that direction."

Eva shrugged. "No idea. We don't go over there on our rides."

Alex hadn't thought about the over the hill rule in years. He smiled a little as he remembered Pops drilling it into his head. Stay in the valley but never, ever go over the hill. Surely that was because he was small and Pops wanted to keep Alex in his line of sight, right? "Let's go check it out."

"Okay." Eva shrugged, and they hopped off the log.

Alex spotted some deer tracks. "Look, deer."

"How do you know it's deer?" she asked, and they chatted about animal tracks. He'd never been this comfortable and relaxed with someone he barely knew. It was nice.

When they got to the top of the hill, they paused. The land rolled in gentle waves, and it was beautiful in the light of the full moon. They could see for miles.

"Wow," Eva said, sounding breathless.

"I know." Something caught Alex's eye. "What's that?" He pointed at a black circle on the ground in the valley below.

She followed his finger to where he was pointing. "A shadow I think."

"From what?" They both glanced around. There were no trees growing near the dark shape and all the surrounding grass was dead.

"I'm not sure," Eva admitted, squinting into the dark.

"Let's check it out."

"Why?"

"Because it's strange and I'm curious. Don't you want to know what it is?"

Eva stared back at her grandparents' house and watched

the last light go out. "If we keep going, you'll have to give me a ride home when we get back."

"Deal." He didn't bother to hide the excitement in his voice.

They started down the hill, and she stumbled over a clod of dirt. He tried to catch her, but they both tumbled over, and she landed on him. "Oof, sorry about that."

Her face was inches from his. To his surprise, she laughed as she shoved herself up and wiped the dirt off her hands. "Sorry? Yes, please. Next time you save me from falling all the way down a hill, please shield the blow even more with your own body."

The sarcasm in her voice made him laugh. "I'll do my best."

They walked again and for about the millionth time in his life, Alex was glad they didn't have poisonous spiders or rattle snakes in this part of Nebraska. Out west, they wouldn't be able to walk through tall grass in the dark, but here they were safe.

A wave of desperation, darkness, and fear washed over Alex with a suddenness that almost knocked him off his feet. It was palpable. He could taste the fear. It was metal in his mouth. "Do you... do you feel that?" he asked, trying to catch his breath.

She was out of breath and dropped to her knees. "Yes, what is it?"

He crouched beside her. "I'm not sure. Are you okay?"

"I just..." She fumbled in her pocket for something and pulled out the same kind of inhaler Alex had seen the guys at practice using. After a few puffs and deep breaths, she moved to get up, and he put his arm underneath of hers, pulling her to her feet.

The air rippled around them with an energy that pulsed through his body. It reminded him of when you stood too close to the speakers at a huge concert. The hair on his arms stood up with a static charge of its own.

He noticed Eva's cross necklace. It was glowing a deep orange ember the color of a flame or a hot coal. "Your necklace! Is it burning you?"

She glanced down, touching the crucifix where it rested between her collarbones. "What the...?" She trailed off. "No, it's cool to the touch."

On instinct, Alex reached out to touch it. She was right. It was normal. He realized he was touching her and pulled his arm back, turning toward the dark shape. It was still far away, but it pulsed as if calling to him. He tried to put one foot in front of the other to move toward it, but it was like dredging through quicksand rather than the short prairie grass.

"We should go back," Eva said over the throbbing hum in his ears.

"I need to know what it is. You can wait here if you want." He tried to walk toward the strange shadow on the ground, but it was zapping his energy. Eva rolled her eyes and walked with him, one hand still on the crucifix. She made faster progress than him and he noticed when he walked in her wake it got easier.

The shadow on the ground appeared to get bigger as they drew closer. It was a dense darkness that was roiling like water as it boils. Smoke puffed up through the air and with it the worst smell he'd ever experienced. It reminded him of week-old manure and the worst body odor ever mixed with the smell of sulfur. Alex covered his nose with his shirt, but it did nothing to mask the smell.

Chapter Sixteen

Power radiated from the necklace where it rested on Eva's skin. Evil surrounded her, but somehow the cross emanated power that gave her a bubble of safety.

Alex was pale beside her, and she wondered if they should go back. But something told her he wasn't giving up until he found out what was down there, and she wasn't staying back alone with this creepiness lurking. As they drew closer, she stared at the dark shadow that emanated the evil. Whatever it was, it couldn't be good for them. That was obvious.

"Okay, let's go back," Alex finally said, and she didn't bother to hide the relief on her face. Together, they trudged toward the top of the hill, one foot in front of the other. Eva wanted to run as fast as she could away from the creepy dark hole, but it had zapped all her energy. Still, every step she took got easier, and finally they made it to the top of the hill.

"That was wild."

"I've never seen anything like that, and your necklace was glowing like crazy. Where'd you get that?"

"It was my great, great—I don't know how many greats—Grandma Lucy's. Maybe it's magic or something."

"Maybe it's blessed."

"What?" Eva walked beside him down the hill toward the creek. Russell had said something similar.

"An item can be blessed if a priest says a special prayer over it. It makes the evil uncomfortable to be around the blessed item because it's holy. Our teacher told us about it in our Wednesday night church classes."

Eva had never heard of blessing things. "Is it normal for blessed stuff to glow?"

"No." He laughed, and it made her feel dumb.

"Well, how'm I supposed to know?"

"Sorry, I forgot you're not Catholic."

"Well, not everyone in this town is." She was tired of not knowing stuff. Tired of the dreams and the weird things happening to them. She was just plain tired. But she shouldn't have snapped at him. It wasn't nice, and she'd already been hard on him with the rejection after school. With how nice he was being tonight, she felt a little bad about that. They walked for a bit in the quiet while she worked up the nerve to apologize. "Sorry." She snuck a quick glance at him. "It's not your fault."

"What's not my fault?"

"All of this. What's happening to us."

A smirk spread across his face. "I agree. It wasn't the first date I had in mind."

She bopped his arm. "This is *not* a first date."

"Oh, that's right, you already shot me down for that." He smirked.

She cringed. "Yea, sorry about that, too. Not the saying no part. I meant that. But I could have been nicer. I'm just. It's stressful right now, you know?"

"I do."

Without thinking, she said, "Well, maybe you should ask again sometime."

"Some time like now?" His smile made Eva's heart pick up speed.

"Better not push your luck anymore tonight, Romeo." Eva smiled at him to soften the blow of her words this time, but she had no intention of dating anyone from this town.

That night, Eva remembered to say the St. Michael prayer before she went to sleep. In fact, she said it twice for good measure. She woke up the next morning to a text from Jai'Lune saying she was coming over. Eva pushed herself up in bed and rubbed her eyes. Light was pouring into her room, and her clock said ten. It was the second good night's sleep she'd had in a row.

Eva texted Jai'Lune to come back to her room when she got there. She let Flip out and headed to the bathroom. When she turned on the light, the bulb burned out. This was getting old. She made a mental note to ask mom to buy a box of lightbulbs. Maybe she should change all the bulbs in the house and see if that helped?

Jai'Lune was sitting on her bed when Eva came back. "Hey, whatcha doing?" she said with an energy Eva couldn't match.

"Still waking up." She squinted, one eye closed, and gave Jai'Lune her best sleepy pirate look.

"Well… how are you doing?"

So much had happened since Eva met Russell. It was as if days had passed in the few hours since Jai'Lune dropped her off at her grandparents' house. "I'm okay. Still processing, I think. But some creepy stuff happened last night after you dropped me off." Eva told Jai'Lune about the shadow hole she found with Alex.

"That's dark, Eva."

"Tell me about it. I wish I knew what it was, you know? How is something out there in a field so close to town and no one's talking about it? I wonder if anyone else knows it's there."

"Be careful. You don't want to go messing with stuff you don't understand. This sort of thing might be more than you and Alex want to get in the middle of, especially on top of the weird dreams and everything else you're dealing with."

"I know. It's just—two super weird things I don't understand are happening with the dreams and finding the shadow hole. I can't help but wonder if they're connected."

"Maybe." Jai'Lune glanced at her phone and stood up. "Oh, I didn't know it was getting this late. I gotta go."

Eva was jolted. She assumed they'd be hanging out all day. "Where are you going?"

"We're going to the city to shop. Want to come with?"

"I would but..."

"I know, I know... except for your mortal hate for all things shopping."

"Exactly, have fun! If I give you some money, can you pick me up a couple of shirts? I'd get whatever you told me to, anyway. But remember, nothing too crazy. I'm no fashion queen like you."

Jai'Lune rolled her eyes, then smiled. "Oh, Eva. I'm unique, not a fashion queen. If you understood fashion at all, you'd know that."

Eva stuck out her tongue at Jai'Lune the way she had when they were five and dug some money out of her nightstand. Jai'Lune snatched it from her. "I got you, girl."

Chapter Seventeen

Alex couldn't sleep after finding the weird shadow hole. He lay awake for hours trying to calm down, but his mind was humming a mile a minute. Finally, he gave up and scrolled on his phone. Alex pulled up the group chat with his international basketball team. It was 9 a.m. in England and one guy messaged, "Do you lot ever have strange dreams? Ones that keep coming back and won't go away?"

Alex sat up in bed and typed back. "Sometimes. What are your dreams about?"

"Tornados." Alex almost dropped the phone. *No way.* Was it spreading? Or had it been going on the whole time?

"How long have you had them?" He paused before hitting send. Alex didn't want to be a crazy interrogator. He hit the backspace and typed, "Oh man, that's not fun. How long have they bothered you?"

"About three months now." Dread stabbed Alex's heart because that's right when his dreams began. Was this happening all over the world? He put his phone down. Maybe it was bigger than he'd ever imagined. And more evil. He shivered, thinking of that black shadow hole they'd seen in the valley. Whatever this was, it wasn't going away. Not without a fight.

~

At 3 a.m. Alex woke up in a sweat, and his arms and legs weighed a thousand pounds. He tried to move, but he couldn't. His heart was racing with fear. Alex tried to shout for his mom, but he couldn't open his mouth. He screamed in his mind, wanting to cry but unable to. Was this another attack? Dark shadows formed in the periphery of his vision and began moving closer from all directions.

"God, if you're there, help me!" A bright white light burst from the center of Alex's room, filling every corner. The suppressive weight released Alex. He curled into a ball and lay there shivering, wondering what had just happened. His heart was racing, and Alex forced himself to count his breaths the way he did when he was running. After a few minutes, his heart stopped trying to leap out of his chest.

Alex saw a glint of something on the floor. He squinted, focusing his eyes, and realized it was the crucifix his mom and dad gave him for his first communion. It must have fallen off his dresser. He hopped out of bed, grabbed it and hopped back into bed, clutching the smooth wooden surface and cold metal figure of Jesus. His room was freezing, but the cross was warm in his hand. He fell asleep and slept for the rest of the night.

~

Alex awoke still clutching the crucifix. He set it on his nightstand and turned off his alarm. Groaning, he rolled over, rubbing the sleep from his eyes. All he wanted was to go back to sleep, but he had weights in twenty minutes. He dragged himself out of bed and splashed cold water on his face, pulled on his gym shorts and t-shirt, grabbed his keys and headed out the door.

As Alex was walking up to the school, he passed a guy on the sidewalk who was leaving. They said hello and Alex kept walking. But there was something odd about the man. He was huge and muscular, but that wasn't the most striking thing about him. There was something in the man's eyes that made him seem a thousand years old, even though he couldn't have been more than twenty.

Alex turned around to watch the guy walk away and saw his body was shimmering like a lake reflecting the sun's light. Alex couldn't focus his eyes on the guy. As he was watching, the guy disappeared into thin air. Alex tripped on his own feet and about fell over. He shook his head and blinked. Closed his eyes and opened them fast. But the guy was gone. Vanished.

Was he hallucinating, or did that just happen? He didn't know, and both possibilities were horrible in their own way. Alex jogged the remaining few feet to the school and threw open the glass door. He was shaken up, but hearing the familiar roar of the radio, guys talking, and weights clinking helped calm him. At least the weight room was something he understood, unlike all this weird spiritual stuff. "You alright Smith?" His coach asked. "You look like you just saw a ghost."

Maybe he had. "Something like that, Coach. Just glad to be here."

The coach bunched his eyebrows and patted him on the back. "Okay, Alex. We're glad you're here too."

After weights, Alex texted Grace. 'Hey, can we meet at the church tonight? Eva and I might have found something.'

'Sure.' She texted back right away.

'Okay, can you ask Eva? I don't have her number.' Two seconds later, another text came through from Grace with Eva's number. He'd worked out about a million scenarios in his head how he could ask Eva for her number and here it was, easy as that.

Grace texted, 'Do a group text with her. That'll be easier.' Man, some girls were bossy.

Alex typed and deleted the text ten times before finally settling on something simple. 'Hey, can you guys meet me at the church after practice tonight? I think we have a lot to talk about.'

He hit send and a few seconds later Eva responded, 'Who is this?' *Oh boy.*

'This is Alex. Grace gave me your number, sorry.'

'Oh, okay, what time?'

Alex hoped she wasn't mad. '7?'

'K.'

When Alex pulled into the parking lot, Eva's and Grace's cars were already there. He pushed open the church door and walked in, pausing a moment to let his eyes adjust to the dim light. Grace and Eva were sitting in the same pew as last time.

"Hey," he said.

"Hey, Alex," Grace said, and Eva smiled at him. *That was different.* "What's up?" Grace asked.

"Well, Eva and I might have found something. Do you want to tell her about it?" he asked Eva.

"Sure." Eva told Grace the story of finding the black shadow hole. He noticed she left out the part about her crying beside the creek.

"I couldn't sleep after we found the black hole, or whatever it is, so I was on my phone," he continued. "I play on some international teams and the guys come from England and stuff. One of them was messaging the group, asking if anyone ever had strange dreams. It turns out he's having the same dreams as us."

Eva's and Grace's eyes both got big. "What?" Grace shouted, then covered her mouth, as if remembering she was in a church.

"This is not just a Marysburg thing or a random girl in California. I think it's bigger than that. And there's more."

"More?" Grace groaned.

"Have you guys seen anything strange?"

"Strange how?" Eva asked. He told them about the shadows and light in his room and the shimmery guy that disappeared.

"Yes! Thank you! I thought I was going crazy," Grace said. "You know how I wait tables at Ellie's Cafe sometimes on the weekends? Well, I had this guy come in a few weeks back. As he paid his bill, he got all serious and said, 'You need to listen to the dreams, Grace. Pay attention, they're telling you something.'

"I stood there, like, excuse me? I'd told no one about the dreams at that point. There was no way he could know. Later, I wished I'd asked him what he meant or how he knew. But I just stood there and watched him walk out the door."

Eva squinted her eyes as if this intrigued her. "What'd he look like?" she asked.

"What you'd expect a person around here to look like. Kinda familiar even. He had on jeans, a flannel shirt and a navy blue jacket. I don't know . . . normal. He was solid though, not shimmery the way the guy you talked about was, Alex. He looked strong too."

"What is it, Eva?" Grace asked, and Alex realized Eva's eyes were open wide again.

"It's just when Grace said 'fight,' it made me think of

something. One night, I heard metal clicking on metal in my living room. The sound made me think of two swords clashing in battle. My dog even heard it. When I met Russell, he said something about spiritual attacks, too."

"What else did your dad say?" Grace asked. "Anything that could help us?"

"I don't think so. It was mostly getting-to-know-you stuff," she said, tapping her foot up and down as if she was uncomfortable talking about it.

"Well, what did he say about the spiritual attacks?" Grace prodded.

"Grace, maybe she doesn't want to talk about it," Alex said.

"No, it's fine," Eva responded. "He didn't say much. I kind of freaked out at that point and bolted."

"Well, do you think you could go back and ask?"

"Grace," Alex said again, wishing she'd stop. It was obvious Eva was uncomfortable with the whole situation. They were lucky she'd said anything at all. Grace shot a glare at him that said *shut up.*

Eva fidgeted with her necklace. "I don't know, maybe?"

"Do you think we could go with you?" Grace pressed. "I need some answers."

"I know. I think we all do. Let me think about it, okay?"

"Sure," Grace said. Had she hit her limit of pushiness? *Was that even possible?*

"Do you guys have holy water?" Grace asked, holding up a small plastic bottle with a gold cross embossed on the front.

"No," they said in unison, and Eva stared at Alex in surprise.

"You don't have holy water? Aren't you Catholic?"

"Yea, but most Catholics don't have a bottle of holy water sitting around. What would we even do with it?"

"Uh, you use it, dummy! If you get scared, you can splash

some around your room or your house and say, 'I bless this house in the name of Jesus Christ.' It keeps the evil away."

"And how's that working out for you?" Alex pressed. His time to be pushy.

"Well, I haven't gotten attacked in my living room the way Eva did and so far, my bedroom's safe, other than the dreams. How about your house, Alex?"

He remembered how afraid he was when he woke up with the weight on his chest and the shadow figures in his room. He shrugged, unwilling to give her the satisfaction of being right, even if she might be.

"That's what I thought. Here, I got a bottle for all of us. Mom has these sitting around in droves." She handed them each a little plastic bottle with a gold cross on the front. "I filled them up already from the holy water container at the front of the church." She pointed toward a silver tank on a stand with a cross on the front. It had a spigot on the front you could turn on like a sink faucet. Alex never noticed it before. "Keep the bottle on your nightstand in case of emergencies, and if you run out, refill the bottle here at church. That's what I did."

She was such a know-it-all. But Alex would try anything if he thought it would help make the creepy things stop. He took the bottle from her and shoved it in the pocket of his letter jacket. Eva took the bottle from Grace and turned it around in her hand. Alex wondered what she was thinking. Maybe that Catholics were even weirder than she thought.

"I'd better get home," Eva said, standing to go.

"Me too," Grace said. "Will you let us know if we can go see your dad with you?"

"Sure," she said, with something close to a glower.

Chapter Eighteen

Eva didn't want them to come with her to see her father. She didn't even know if *she* wanted to see him again. She needed time on her own to process. It's how she operated. Step back from the world, think through it alone, and decide. This was all moving too fast.

She remembered Alex, his hair standing up funny on one side where he kept running his hands through it with worry. His dark brown eyes were tired at the church. And Grace was getting dark circles under her eyes. If Eva could help them, shouldn't she do it?

She picked up her phone and texted Russell, 'Would it be okay if me and some friends come and see you tomorrow night at 8:00? Sorry it's late. I have to work.' She'd be freaking out every moment until they went. Might as well get it over with tomorrow. This would be perfect. She'd be distracted all day at school, plus she had work. Not much time to think.

'Sure, that'd be great!' he texted back almost instantly. He sent another text, 'You want me to make supper again?'

'No, that's okay,' she texted back. As an afterthought she

sent, 'But the chili and cinnamon rolls were delicious, thanks. Where'd you learn to cook that way?'

'I went to culinary school. I was a chef in the city before I came back here.' *Well, wasn't he full of surprises?*

'Cool. Night,' she texted back to wrap it up.

'Sweet dreams,' he responded with a little prayer emoji. *Amen to that.*

Eva texted the group chat with Alex and Grace. 'Hey, Russell said tomorrow night at 8 works.'

'Shoot! We have my brother's piano recital. I can't get out of it,' Grace texted. 'You guys go and let me know what you find out.'

Eva's finger was hovering over the keyboard, trying to think of a fast excuse to get out of going to see Russell alone with Alex. A text came through from him. 'Works for me.'

Dang, she wasn't fast enough. A couple seconds later, on a side message, Alex said, 'I don't know where your dad lives. You want me to pick you up and we can go together?'

Uh, no. I don't want you to go at all. Spare me the awkward time in the car. 'Sure.'

On Tuesday, Eva got to lunch before everyone else and was already at the table eating when someone set their tray down beside her. When she realized it was Alex, her heartbeat picked up a little, annoying her. *Now they were sitting together at lunch?* She cringed. This was going to tick Janet off.

"Hey," he said.

"Hi," Eva said around a mouthful of biscuit.

"We still on for your dad's tonight?"

"Yep."

"You still live on 7th Street across from Mrs. Cotner, right?"

Wow, Eva didn't even think he knew she existed two months ago and now he knew where she lived. "Uh, yes."

"Okay, got it."

The lights flickered. "Did you see that?" Eva asked.

"Yep! It's driving me crazy. We keep running out of lightbulbs."

"Same. But look around, nobody else saw it."

He glanced around the lunchroom and shrugged. "I wonder if it's related to the power outages?"

"What power outages?" Eva asked.

"One guy on that basketball team I told you about said his lights are flickering. The power went out in his neighborhood, and it spread through the entire City of New York. The power company was freaking out because they couldn't figure out what the problem was. Suddenly, the lights came back on. I guess it's happened to a few cities now."

"Weird."

Jai'Lune sat down next to Eva with an eye roll that said, *have we been transported to another planet where we now sit with jocks?*

Eva shrugged her shoulders. She had that creepy sensation she was being watched and glanced around the lunchroom. She saw Janet sitting at a table in the corner, shooting daggers at her and Alex. *Yikes.*

That afternoon when Eva clocked in, Roxie gave her the usual glare. Eva shrugged and Roxie turned to storm off. As she did, Eva saw a horrible, reptilian beast the size of a large dog crawling after her on all fours. *What the heck?* Acting on instinct, she picked up a stack of plastic cups and threw them at the thing. Roxie turned to glare at her. "What are you doing?"

"I, uh, I don't know." The nasty creature was gone.

Roxie stomped off and Eva spent the rest of her shift trying to catch another glimpse of whatever she'd seen, but it was useless. The adrenaline kept her moving, and she finished a little early. She went home and changed, ditching her hairnet and white pants for jeans and a t-shirt just in time to see Alex pull up in front of her house. *Perfect, no time to wait and worry.*

"Hey, how was work?" He asked as she buckled in.

"Good." It was nice of him to remember. "How was practice?"

"Same old, same old. Must be nice to have a job."

"Oh yeah, it's great," she said, not hiding her sarcasm.

He raised one eyebrow, embarrassed. "I just mean, I'd love to have some of my own money."

"You don't work at all?"

"I can't with my sports schedule and camps in summer and everything. I mean, I pick up odd jobs for Pops, but that doesn't count."

"Will you play sports in college?"

"That's the plan. Or at least, that's my dad's plan," he said with an ironic laugh.

"And what do you want to do?"

"I'm over it. I want to be a vet. I wish I could focus on my classes and that's it."

"You like animals?" That surprised her.

"Yea, they're kind of my thing." *Well, they had that in common.*

When they got to Russell's house, he opened the door as they walked up. Smart guy, don't give her the opportunity to chicken out before she got inside.

"Hi. This is Alex."

"Nice to meet you, sir," Alex said. *Geez, lighten up, dork. Who calls people sir anymore?*

"Nice to meet you too, Alex. You can call me Russell."

"Yes sir, I mean, Russell." When Alex laughed, Eva realized for the first time that he was nervous.

Eva and Alex sat on the couch and Russell brought them each a root beer. "How's the week going for you two?"

"Good," they said in unison.

"Are you in the same grade?"

They nodded.

"Nice." Russell gazed at Alex as if he was sizing him up. "You play sports?"

"Yep." Alex nodded.

Eva appreciated that he didn't brag about himself. In fact, he appeared to be as uncomfortable talking about himself as she usually felt when the conversation spotlight was on her. She turned her attention to Russell. *Time to get to it.* "You know how we were talking about the dreams last time I was here?"

He nodded, glancing at Alex.

"Well, Alex is having them too." Eva paused. "Our friend Grace is too. She's Spencer O'Donnell's daughter."

"Is that right?" Russell's mouth dropped open, and his head tilted to the side in bewilderment.

Alex found his voice now that he wasn't the topic of conversation. "People in other parts of the world are having them too. The problem is that none of us know what they mean."

Russell took forever to respond. In the silence, the story from the Bible about Joseph popped into Eva's head. She felt like the king when he asked Joseph to interpret his dreams. Maybe Russell could be her Joseph.

Chapter Nineteen

Alex shifted on the couch. He had the need to move as they waited to see what Russell would say. After an eternity, Russell took a deep breath and spoke. "Well, I've done some research over the years and a lot of praying, trying to figure out what the dreams mean. From what I understand, they are God's way of reaching out to us, warning us of an impending evil attack."

Eva shuttered and scooted closer to Alex. She glanced up at him as if embarrassed when she realized what she'd done. He smiled at her, not minding the touch of her arm on his.

She turned her attention back to Russell. "What kind of evil attack?"

"Well, the angels and demons battle in the spiritual world all the time. That's no secret." Alex nodded. "What humans don't know, or at least most people don't know, is that we can join the spiritual battle."

"How?" Alex asked. He imagined slaying demons left and right with his great grandpa's Knights of Columbus sword Mom kept stashed in their attic. He had wanted to learn how to use that sword since he was little.

"Well, there are prayers," Russell said. Alex sat back, a little deflated. Prayer didn't sound as fun as an actual battle. "You can ask God for strength or to give the angel's power. You can reject lies and spot when the devil is tricking you, so you don't go along with it. There are lots of big and little ways you can join the battle."

"Similar to any other battle, sometimes one side is winning and then the other pulls ahead for a bit. When humankind isn't doing our part, it's harder for the angels. They get worn down. That's when... things can get interesting."

"Interesting how?" Eva asked and although Alex was curious, there was also a part of him that didn't want to know.

"Well, to put it plainly, the battle that's raging all around us in the invisible spiritual world can break into the physical world. Then it becomes visible—something we see or experience. People who are the most sensitive to the spiritual realm will realize what's happening first. Little glimpses of the battle will leak through." Alex thought of the time he was attacked in his truck on the way home from practice. Goosebumps formed on his arms. Maybe he knew a little too well what Russell was talking about. "Eventually, it can spread. Everyone can see it, and it becomes too obvious to ignore. Darkness can pour into our world. Evil."

"How does it break through?" Alex asked. Maybe that's not what mattered. Maybe what he needed to know was how to get rid of it.

"Humankind plays a part in the battle. We can strengthen the angels with our prayers, or we can show the evil the upper hand with our choices. When we show the evil our cooperation by doing something we shouldn't or believing its lies, little holes get poked in the veil separating the visible and invisible world. Then evil pours through."

"A wisp at first. But sometimes that hole in the veil joins with another little hole and it gets a little bigger. Over time, these grow larger and larger. Sometimes giant holes are torn by a single horrendous evil such as killing children. The wider the holes, the more likely they are to create a portal that attracts evil and lets it enter the world without resistance."

"So, the holes are getting bigger?" Eva asked.

"I think so, yes."

"We're weakening the angels' front line," Alex thought aloud. "They can only defend so much before they have to fall back and reestablish their defenses." His dad had made them sit through enough war movies to know that much.

"Exactly." Russell nodded. "The angels are trying to hold the evil off as long as they can to give us more time, but the spiritual world is in great turmoil right now. It's only a matter of time before the darkness spills into our world."

Alex shivered, wondering what that meant. Russell barreled on. "The terror in the dreams is the feeling evil is about to come through. Terror is how we perceive what's about to happen with our human senses." Russell paused. "And there's not a lot of time before we see the evil break through in a big way. In fact, it's probably already begun."

"What makes you say that?" Alex asked.

"The tornados, for one. There used to be two. Now there are three. The attacks I'm seeing bust through. It's escalating."

"What do you suggest we do?" Eva asked, sounding distant.

"That's where it gets complicated. What I do know is that we're stronger together. When you trust the people you're with and pray with them, it messes up the enemies' tactics. It makes us stronger and the enemy weaker. Trust and togetherness are the keys. When your mom and I lost that, the evil got the upper hand in our battle the last time around."

Eva was hugging herself. Alex wished he could put his arm around her to comfort her. "What happens if we can't keep the evil out?" she asked.

"It will be as nothing the world has ever seen. There's a special place in hell, kind of like a supermax prison, where the worst of the worst demons have been banished by exorcisms and prayer over the centuries. But I believe they'll be released to enter our world through the gates of darkness humans have opened for them."

"They'll spread their darkness through the entire world in a physical way and bring with them chaos, panic, and death. The evil will no doubt be desperate to cause as much damage as possible before it's pushed out of our world again by the angels."

"Wait a minute," Eva said. "If the demons are at war with God, and we're the ones letting them in, why are they coming after us?" It was a good question.

"The evil doesn't care about us. Its sole mission is to hurt God. Since we're God's children and he loves us more than anything, Satan knows hurting us hurts God."

"What about the people who don't believe in God? Will the evil leave them alone?" *Asking for a friend?*

Russell paused and took a deep breath. "It's kind of like with you and me, Eva. Even if you choose not to have a relationship with me, I would still be your father. As your father, I love you whether or not you ever choose to speak with me, acknowledge my existence, or get to know me."

"It's that way with God. We are all his children. He is our father, whether or not we choose to speak to him, acknowledge his existence or have a relationship with him. And he loves us more than we can comprehend. Even if we don't love him back, when the evil hurts us, it hurts God."

Alex nodded. "That makes sense." Eva pushed her lips together as if she wasn't convinced.

"If God's all-powerful, why doesn't he stop all of it?" Eva pressed.

"Because he wants to give us the freedom to choose. He

doesn't force his love on us. We can accept his love or reject it. Empower the angel with our prayers or empower the demons with our choices. Evil doesn't have any power over us unless we let it. You get to choose what to believe. You get to choose what you take and what you get rid of in this life."

"But if we all have choices, out of everyone in the world, why are *we* the ones having the dreams? Why us?" Eva asked.

"Well, Eva, it's your spiritual heritage." Alex and Eva exchanged glances. They'd talked about that by the creek the other night. "We all have a physical heritage, but we can also have a spiritual heritage. For our family, it began back in 1887 when our ancestors came from Chicago to claim the very farmland we're on right now. They could get it for free if they planted and cared for trees. In fact, your great-great-great-grandmother Lucy and her family planted that grove of trees out there. She's the one who owned that necklace I gave you." Eva touched the necklace. Alex noticed it had become her habit.

"That's your physical heritage. But on his deathbed, my father told me about our spiritual heritage, and that explained a lot. Back in 1887, when our family was first here, Lucy and her two friends found something on the land. Something evil. They called it the gates of darkness because they believed it was a doorway to hell."

Alex leaned back. Eva raised one eyebrow. No doubt they were both thinking about the shadow hole they had found in the valley the other night.

"When Lucy and her friends found the gates of darkness and encountered the evil, it awakened in them the ability to be more sensitive and aware of the spiritual world. I always figured it was a gift from God to help protect them. Since then, descendants from every generation of those original children who discovered the gates of darkness have received the same spiritual perception." Russell shrugged, and it reminded

Alex of a gesture he'd seen Eva make several times. "It's why Eva's mom and I had the dreams. Why you are having them now. People in town call us the Dream Havers."

"Are Eva and I related?" Alex blurted the question, shoving down a moment of panic.

Russell chuckled. "No, there were several kids who discovered the gates of darkness." Alex sighed, grateful Eva wasn't his cousin.

Another thought hit Alex. "Do you think there are more out there? More gates of darkness, I mean."

"Absolutely. Don't people sin all around the world?" Russell asked. It made sense. *Why did he ask such a stupid question?*

"I think that's why the dreams and visions are spreading. The gates are getting wider around the world. Have you seen the lights flicker? Heard about the power outages across the globe?"

Eva nodded and Alex said, "My friend in New York said the power companies can't figure it out."

"That's because they're looking in the wrong world. I'm afraid the invisible battle has already begun to reach into the visible world."

"That's why I'm back." Russell turned to Eva, as if to implore her to understand. "One day, a couple of months ago, I was praying for you. I felt a powerful surge, as if you were in danger. It kept happening every time I sat down to pray for you."

"I had a sense you were having the dreams, too. You're about the age I was when it began. I couldn't stand the thought of letting you go through it alone. I knew how vulnerable that could make you to the attacks. It's the reason I'm here. I want to help you."

Russell leaned forward and stared Eva in the eye. "Have

you two experienced anything unusual? Other than the dreams, I mean."

Eva and Alex nodded. Russell leaned back with a quick nod. Concern crossed his face like clouds moving past the sun. "Have they increased in frequency or intensity?" Russell asked, as if he was a doctor at a checkup.

"I guess," Eva said, holding her hands palms up but not offering more information.

Russell stared at Eva with his intent brown eyes matching hers. "That's what I was afraid of. The tension is building. I'm afraid everything is coming to a head. We might have less time than I thought."

"And the evil will come at you two hard now in the beginning stages, when it perceives you as weak. Like the young of a herd, you're spiritual infants, unaware of how to protect yourself. It's the easiest time for the evil to attack you. A lot of the tactics will be around crippling you with fear and anxiety. It's trying to get you to block out the dreams and God. The evil will be desperate to stop you now because it knows how powerful you'll be if you learn to join the battle."

"If that's what's going on, what do you think we should do about it?" This guy had put a lot of time and effort into investigating what was going on. Surely, he'd also spent at least a little time figuring out how they could defend themselves. Alex was desperate to make the dreams and everything else stop. He'd probably try about anything. Maybe he should be careful though. Was it smart to trust just anybody? What did he even know about this guy? He was Eva's father. Was that enough?

"I believe it starts small. The Bible says, 'Whoever can be trusted with very little can also be trusted with much.' If everyone having the dreams reaches out to the people in their local area, the entire world could be warned. We could take up arms with the Word of God, which is our sword. Pray. Lean on each other. That weakens the evil."

"I'm willing to help get this going in any way I can, but I'm not sure if partnering with me will be what's best for you. In the town's eyes, I'm a no-good drunk who got your mom pregnant and took off. It might be better if I supported you from afar. What we need is someone in the public eye we can trust who is well-liked and respected in this town. Someone people will listen to. Know anybody like that?"

Alex and Eva sat in silence, thinking hard. "How about my priest?" Alex asked.

"It'd be better if it was a regular person. Even if the priest believed us, the Catholic Church moves slowly. They won't give their stamp of approval on anything unless it's been thoroughly investigated. That could take years, and we don't have that kind of time. Everything indicates the darkness will be here soon."

Eva shook her head. "I'm not sure. I mean, there's lots of good people but I don't know if they'd be listened to about something this crazy."

"That's okay," Russell said with a shrug. "This can be your first lesson in trusting God to provide. Pray he will send someone to help you, and keep your eyes and ears open. You'll know when you find them."

"It kinda feels like we're fighting a losing battle," Eva admitted. "The people in our dreams never listen to us. Isn't that a sign the people in real life won't listen, either?"

"It won't be easy," Russell admitted. "God never promises easy." Alex nodded. Eva pulled her shoulders forward and together as if she wanted to disappear.

The conversation was winding down, and Alex stood to stretch his legs. They were still sore from weights that morning. He shook Russell's hand. "Thank you. You've given us a lot to think about."

"I hope so. Come back anytime."

Eva gave Russell a weird half smile. Then she and Alex stepped out into the night together. Alex was glad Eva didn't come alone tonight. If he was being honest, he was glad he wasn't out in the dark alone too. After what they'd heard, the darkness was menacing.

Eva was quiet in the car and Alex wondered what she was thinking and what he should say to break the silence. Why not try the truth? "That was intense."

"Tell me about it," Eva responded, letting out a long breath.

"Do you believe it? I mean, do you think it's real?"

"I don't know," Eva admitted. "It sounds crazy, right? But we're having these dreams and stuff and that's crazy. The answer might be crazy too."

"Thanks for letting me tag along tonight. I know that wasn't easy with you guys just having met and all."

"No problem," Eva said as they pulled up to her house.

Her hand was on the door, but he couldn't let her go without telling her how he felt. "I like hanging out with you, Eva. Even when we are talking about crazy stuff." He grinned. "I hope someday I can take you out on a real first date."

She paused, and an eternity passed before she answered. Alex panicked. Maybe he shouldn't have said anything. He didn't want to ruin whatever chance he had by being an idiot. Maybe this was why he didn't have any friends. *Read the room, man!* He tried to backpedal. "Or not, that's totally cool."

"No," Eva said, and smiled at him. "I think maybe I might like that." She gave him a smile that made his heart stop. He smiled back at her, realizing it had been a long time since he'd been this happy. "Night Romeo."

Chapter Twenty

Wow, so that just happened. A weird feeling of bliss was swirling in her head along with the strange stuff Russell told them. She was in her living room, leaning against the front door again, when someone pounded on the door. Eva jumped half a foot and adrenaline swept through her. She was home alone. What should she do?

She flipped on the porch light and moved the curtain aside a fraction of an inch to peek outside. Alex was standing in the center of the light with a crazed look in his eye. Eva watched as he flailed his arms, swatting at his back like a person being chased by a swarm of bees. "Eva! Help! Get it off me! Get it off!"

"Alex?" Eva flung open the door, and he ran into her living room, still screaming. "Help, Eva! It's on my back!"

"What? What's on your back?" Eva asked, her heart beating fast. She felt urgent but powerless. She couldn't see anything on his back. The lights flickered off and on, off and on.

"Can't you see it? Oh Jesus, help me! Help!"

At those words, a blindfold was removed from Eva's eyes.

She could see a horrible, ravenous dog clinging to Alex's back, lunging for his throat with fierce persistence. The creature, made of darkness and shadow, was foaming at the mouth, emanating rage. Again and again, Alex swatted the dog away, but it was obvious he was getting tired. And the dog was getting better and better at avoiding his blows from the awkward angle behind his back.

"Hit it, Eva! Hit it with something!" She grabbed the fireplace poker and swung. The old metal collided with the side of the beast's head. It yelped and fell to the living room floor.

Taking advantage of the beast's surprise, Alex kicked it. All his fear and anger seemed to pour into each blow. The beast snarled with hate. Eva thought it might rally and come at them again. Alex pulled his foot back for another kick. Its eyes rolled back, and it burst into orange embers. The grotesque confetti drifted down. They watched as the embers turned to ashes and dissolved. Alex and Eva stared at the empty spot on the floor, a sulfuric smell burning the air that reminded her of the smell in the valley. She stared at Alex with terror in her eyes, "Wha... what was that?"

"I have no idea. Are you okay?" He pulled Eva into a hug, and she hugged him back, grateful for something to hold on to. "Oh my gosh, I'm so sorry I brought it here. I... I didn't think." He released her and paced the room.

"I was backing out of your driveway and suddenly this thing was on me. I started swinging at it and threw my truck into park. I was out there in your yard running around swatting at it like a crazy person," he trailed off. "I'm sorry, Eva. I shouldn't have put you in danger." He leaned over, holding the arm of the couch, trying to catch his breath.

Eva put her hand on his back. Then she giggled. He glanced up at her as if she might be losing her mind. Maybe she was. "I'm sorry. I'm just picturing you running around like an insane person in my yard. It's funny, okay?"

He cracked a smile, and the tension broke a little in the room. "Yeah, I guess it is a little." They could laugh or they could cry. This felt better.

"Oh gosh, you're bleeding," Eva said and stepped closer to peer at a spot on his neck where the creature's teeth must have broken the skin. Alex touched it and when he pulled his hand away blood glistened on his fingers. His eyes rolled back in his head, and he collapsed on the floor.

For a millisecond, Eva stared at him uncertain what to do. She dropped to her knees and shook his shoulder. "Alex! Alex?" Had the creature's bite been poisonous? Was he dead? Could the evil spirits kill them? *Should she call the ambulance?* She grabbed her phone, but at that moment Alex's eyes opened groggily.

She watched his face register where he was, and he sat up. "Sorry, I uh... don't do well with blood."

Eva let out a loud guffaw of relief and slapped his shoulder. "I guess not! You scared me. I thought you were *dead*!"

His face flushed. "Sorry. Ever since I was young, I pass out at the sight of blood. I don't... I don't know why."

The big, tough guy had a tiny weakness... blood. Weird. "It's no big deal," Eva said, pulling him to his feet. "I mean, I'm just glad you didn't die. That would have really messed up the rug." When he didn't respond, she said, "I'm kidding! Sorry. Trying to lighten the mood." In that moment, she realized how utterly exhausted and destroyed he was. "Are you sure you're okay?"

He stared down at the floor and said, "I have to be." He paused, then said, "I gotta go. Weights early tomorrow."

"At least let me get you a bandage before you leave. I don't want you to glance in the rearview mirror and pass out while you're driving."

He smirked. "I guess that would be bad."

"Be right back, sit down." She pointed to her couch and

jogged to the bathroom to grab some supplies. When she got back, Alex was leaning his head on the back of the couch like he was sleeping. She sat down beside him with the brown bottle of hydrogen peroxide, a rag, and some bandages. He opened his eyes and sat up.

Eva dumped some hydrogen peroxide on the rag and tried to be gentle, not her strong suit, as she dabbed at the bite marks. She tried to get as much blood off as she could. Then she put some antibiotic ointment on one of the big bandages and put it over the spot, her fingers brushing the warmth of the skin on his neck. He watched her face while she worked and when she was done, she glanced up into his deep brown eyes. "There, much better."

"Thank you, truly, Eva." His voice sounded husky and she could feel herself blushing as a warmth spread through her.

"It's no big deal." As he left, she watched him jog to his pickup. The fear of what happened mixed with her feelings for Alex, stirring up in a strange storm of emotions. But she was too tired to make sense of it right now.

At school the next day, Eva was a zombie. Alex sat by her at lunch, looking as dazed as she felt. A few girls saw them sitting together and whispered. A couple even pointed. She was too tired to care. She ignored them and glanced at Alex. "Doing okay?" She noticed a skin-toned small bandage covering the spot on his neck.

He gave her a weak smile. "I guess. How about you?"

"About the same."

Jai'Lune sat down on the other side of Eva, and they were a safe fortress of protection surrounding her.

Chapter Twenty-One

Alex was still creeped out as he pulled his car into the church parking lot that evening. Grace had called another meeting. This was getting to be a regular thing. She wanted to know what they'd found out from Russell, and he didn't blame her. They all wanted answers.

Eva pulled into the parking lot right after him, and they walked toward the church together. Alex had the impulse to grab her hand. He needed something to hold on to. *Too soon.* He warned himself. Don't be weird. But somehow, in all the craziness, she was a steady constant in the storm.

The guilt and embarrassment of what happened at her house the other evening washed over him. Again. He'd been fighting it all day. How could he have brought that *thing* to her doorstep? "I'm sorry about yesterday. Man, what was that?"

"I don't know, but it's freaking me out."

"Me too. You saw it, right? When you hit it, that's because you could see it too."

She nodded. "After you said those words."

"Huh?"

"You talked to God."

He didn't even remember what he'd said. He wished he did. "You've got a pretty good swing. You might have a baseball career in your future."

"Ha. That'd be the day. How was practice?"

"Okay. Big game tomorrow." At least on the football field, everything made sense. It always had, and it gave him an outlet he needed right now. But sometimes he still wanted to curl up in a ball in his room and wait until all this craziness had passed. He never thought he'd wish to go back to the boring, ordinary days before all this began, but he did. Fear could do strange things to you.

Grace zipped into the parking lot, parked her tiny red car, and threw open her door. "Oh my gosh, you guys, the creepiest thing happened to me last night."

Alex and Eva glanced at each other and walked toward Grace. "I can't tell you here, though. Let's go inside." She peered around with suspicion as if spies were lurking, and Alex wondered who she could be worried about overhearing them. It was hard to say with Grace.

They sat in their normal pew close to the back, and Grace immediately began talking. "Okay, it was late, about three in the morning. Sometimes I stay up late watching videos on my phone when the house is finally quiet, you know?"

Alex nodded for her to go on.

"I was the only one awake in the house. I went into the bathroom to get a drink and it was like I walked into a trap. I flipped on the light and the lightbulb burned out. This wave of... I don't know, despair... hit me like a toxic gas. The room felt like an evil black hole that could suck all the good out of everything."

"I turned to run, but I couldn't move. I wanted to scream, but I couldn't. So, I prayed in my mind, you know? Whatever it was, it let go of me a little, and I ran into the living room. But it followed me. I dropped to my knees and begged God to protect me. Suddenly it all lifted and everything I'd been feeling was gone." She glanced from Alex to Eva. "Am I losing my mind?"

"Maybe not. We had something similar happen to us." Alex told her the story of the monster and how Eva saved him with the poker.

"But I couldn't see it until Alex prayed."

"Maybe Great Granny was right. We have to pray."

"Maybe," Eva agreed. She told Grace what Russell said about them being stronger together and that they had a spiritual ancestry.

"This has been going on in my family for generations. Why didn't anyone tell me?" She sounded betrayed.

Eva shrugged. "I think they're all too scared. Or hoping it will eventually go away. I mean, I get trying to live a normal life."

"So now we're in some sort of evil war or something?"

"Or something," Alex agreed.

Eva handed Grace the candle. "Russell said to give you this. It's a blessed candle. It will give you light no matter what happens. It sounds like the evil can't blow it out."

Grace took the candle from Eva, hugging it to herself as a child hugs a teddy bear. The silence grew. Suddenly, Grace said, "I have an idea."

Alex and Eva stared at her, waiting for her to go on. "You know Ellie?"

"The one who runs the café?" Eva asked.

"Yes. She's my religion teacher on Wednesday nights, and she's a cousin to my Great Granny Maggie or something. She's totally a mother figure to everyone, you know? Even big biker dudes listen to her and stuff. What if we asked her to help us? I mean, people listen when she talks. If we're gonna warn people, or whatever, maybe they'd listen better if she was helping us."

"Grace, you're a genius!" Eva said.

Alex couldn't explain it if he tried, but somehow in that moment, he knew with absolute certainty Ellie was the one who was meant to help them. "Yes, that feels right."

Finally, maybe they were making some progress. It struck Alex that Russell had told them to pray for someone to help. Could this be an answered prayer?

"I work Saturday. I'll ask her if we can talk after closing. Why don't you guys come to the café around seven?" Grace said in her bossy tone. Still, he had to admit, it was a good plan.

Alex nodded and Eva said, "Okay."

"Great, that's settled. I was thinking we'd come at it as if we have a problem we need help with. We can tell her about the dreams and what Eva's dad and my Great Granny said. What do you think?"

"Makes sense." Thank God he wasn't trying to do this all on his own. Whether it was God or Grace calling the shots, he was glad somebody else was doing it. He wouldn't even know where to begin. They stood to leave and as they walked out, Alex had an idea. "Hey, Eva, can I talk to you for a minute?"

"Okay, see ya," Grace said with a little wave, and she was gone.

Alex could hear the gravel of the parking lot crunch under his shoes as he shifted from foot to foot. "If you, uh, wanted, I could pick you up for Ellie's Saturday. Maybe we could grab a bite at Tasteez afterward."

Eva wrinkled her nose. "What?" He asked, unable to stifle a little laugh at how cute she was.

"I'm just imagining death-by-glare from Janet. Doesn't she work there?"

"Oh true." Gosh, he'd forgotten about that.

"We could call ahead and ask Ellie to make us something to go. It'd give us a good reason for showing up, too."

"Great!" He was surrounded by female masterminds. As Eva drove away, Alex's head spun. Despite all his lack of planning and bumbling, he did it! Why was it so hard? He'd had a girlfriend before. *But Janet did all the pursuing.* He suddenly realized he'd never been the one to ask Janet out. She sauntered up to him one day in the hall and said, "We're going out Saturday. Pick me up at seven."

He'd stuttered, "Okay," and that was that. She'd bossed him around from the moment they first got together. How did he not see it before?

Chapter Twenty-Two

Did she want to hang out with Alex? Jai'Lune was going to freak out when Eva told her what she had just committed to. This was worthy of a call, not a text. She had to hear Jai'Lune's reaction.

"You *what*?" Jai'Lune screamed into the phone. "Oh my gosh, this is epic. Do you realize how epic this is?"

"Pretty epic."

"You should come to the football game with me this Friday. Watch him play. I'm not gonna lie, he's pretty great. And you can hold my music for band. It'll be fun!"

Eva considered. School events weren't her thing, but why pass up a chance to hang out with Jai'Lune? "Okay, if you promise to help me figure out what to wear for my date on Saturday. Deal?"

"Deal! I bought you the perfect shirt to wear. I'll bring it over on Saturday. You're gonna be smokin' hot!"

"If you say so." Eva hung up the phone. A wave of heavy fear hit her hard. It began with a buzzing sound, as if a fly was zooming close to her ears. A deep heaviness weighed on her heart, freezing her in place.

Eva glanced down and saw a giant black snake slowly curling around her legs. Its beady eyes were glowing embers. She tried to step away, but with lightning-fast speed, it synched its body around her legs, and she fell to the floor with a scream.

Eva tried to wiggle free, but each time she did, it coiled tighter around her. Could snakes have facial expressions? Because she was pretty sure this one was sneering at her. Its white teeth glistened, and green slime dripped from its fangs. She peered around, frantic as a rising tide of panic washed over her. Her body flooded with fear and the edges of her vision went dark. Then she saw it. The holy water sitting on her nightstand. She stretched and reached for it, unscrewing the lid with trembling fingers, as the snake slithered higher up her body.

Finally, the lid was off, and Eva splashed a few drops on the snake. She couldn't remember all the words Grace told her to pray, but she could remember one. "Jesus." The sound of it felt as unfamiliar on her lips as it did when she thought of calling Russell, Dad.

As the holy water hit the snake's scales, steam rose from its body. It hissed and recoiled backward, loosening its grip. It was enough for Eva to wiggle her legs free. Her bag was on the bed, loaded with heavy textbooks. She swung it high over her head, the adrenaline making her strong, and brought it crashing down on the stunned snake. She lifted the bag and brought it down again and again. The snake flattened, then burst every seam and sickening ash exploded, raining down where the snake had been.

The smell of sulfur burned Eva's nose. She shivered as she watched the ash dissipate into thin air. Her breath was coming in short bursts and her throat was tight. She grabbed her inhaler from her pocket and took two puffs, trying to calm her breathing. Her heart was still racing, but she could breathe.

She dove into bed and hiked the covers up to her chin, shivering despite the warmth of the blankets.

She stared at the ceiling. What just happened? Russell's words came back to her. *It's only a matter of time before the darkness spills into our world.* Was the snake a wisp of evil making its way through the veil separating their worlds? Eva shuddered and pulled the blankets even tighter around her.

At the football game the next day, there was a spark of excitement in the air. The smell of popcorn and hot dogs lingered as people cheered and the band played. "Maybe I can see why people enjoy sports. It's kinda exciting."

Jai'Lune's mouth dropped open in a look that said *duh. Then* she sprang out of her seat and clapped her gloved hands. "We need a field goal to tie it."

Alex had the ball, and suddenly he threw it up high. It soared down the field, and the crowd was silent. Everyone held their breath, waiting to see if number three would catch the football. As the seconds ticked down to zero, the ball slipped into number three's arms. He turned and ran. The other team chased close behind, but there was no catching him. The crowd erupted as the announcer said, "Touchdown Marysburg!"

"We won! We won!" Jai'Lune jumped up and down. Eva laughed and stood up beside her, joining the celebration. She saw Alex run up to one of his teammates and bump chests in midair.

"Want to go on the field?" Jai'Lune asked.

"What? Why?"

"Seriously, do you live under a rock? To congratulate the players! Maybe Alex will give you a big ole public smackeroo. That'd tick Janet off." Jai'Lune cackled at her own joke.

"Ha." Might as well get the full high school experience, Eva thought as she followed Jai'Lune to the field.

Jai'Lune picked a path toward Colin, and Eva trailed behind her. Alex caught her eye and jogged over.

"You did good! I don't know anything about football, but that last throw was amazing," Eva said.

"Thanks, Eva. Thanks for being here."

Uh-oh, did he think she was there for him? "Jai'Lune invited me. I needed to get out of the house."

He nodded. *Was that disappointment on his face?* "It was fun, though." She didn't want to make him feel bad.

"Really?"

She nodded as Jai'Lune and Colin walked up, and Eva said, "Nice catch Colin."

Colin smacked Alex on the helmet. "I couldn't have done it without this guy."

"Thanks, man." Alex gave him a smile and glanced down. For the first time, Eva realized he was shy. How had she missed that?

"I hate to break up this bromance, but Eva, are you ready to go?" Jai'Lune asked.

Eva nodded.

"See you tomorrow?" There was hope in Alex's eyes and something else—insecurity, maybe?

Eva smiled. "See you tomorrow."

Jai'Lune drove them to Eva's house. "Are you nervous about your date?"

"A little. Okay, a lot. I don't know what I'm doing. This is crazy!" It would be easier to curl up with a good book than deal with these nerves, but life was worth living, wasn't it? Besides, it was good practice for when she dated in college. Now she wouldn't be new to the game.

"Don't worry, I'll come over tomorrow and keep you distracted until Romeo picks you up. Deal?"

"How did you know I call him that?" She'd only ever said that to Alex when they were alone.

"I sensed it. It's obvious, isn't it?" Jai'Lune asked with a laugh.

"I guess." Eva shrugged and Jai'Lune gave her a sideways smile.

~

The next day, Jai'Lune stood back and admired her creation. She'd been giving Eva a makeover for the last thirty minutes and refused to let her get a peek. But now Eva stole a glimpse in the mirror. Her lips were bright red, and her eyes painted with charcoal gray eyeshadow.

"Jai'Lune, I don't know. It's not me."

"You don't even know, do you?"

"Know what?"

Jai'Lune rolled her eyes. "Eva, you're beautiful. Drop-dead-gorgeous even."

"Whatever." Eva rolled her eyes and her cheeks got warm. She hated it when she blushed.

"Your mom was pretty, and you are too. It's crazy you can't see it." Her eyebrows pulled together, and her head tilted in a look of bafflement.

Eva stared at the mirror and pretended she was seeing someone else. Maybe she could see it? She knew she wasn't horrible, but she also couldn't help but notice her eyes were a little too far apart. Her forehead was a little too tall, and what about that zit forming on her right cheek? Jai'Lune's gaze and hands on her hips were commanding a response. "Okay, maybe I'm not that bad."

Jai'Lune must have taken that as a win. "It's a start," she nodded.

~

In an instant, things in the house rattled. Was this another attack? She stared at Jai'Lune to see if she was experiencing it too. "Do you feel that?"

"Uh, kinda impossible to miss." Jai'Lune put her arms out for balance and glanced around, wide-eyed.

If Jai'Lune could feel it, did that mean it wasn't spiritual? It was happening in the real world. *When did it become so hard to tell what was real?* Eva stood up and almost lost her balance. The floor was vibrating and shifting under her feet. "What's happening?"

"I think it's an earthquake. Get in a doorway!" Jai'Lune grabbed Eva's arm and pulled her to the doorway between the living room and kitchen, but by the time they got there, the shaking had already stopped. Everything was calm.

"Did that seriously just happen?" Jai'Lune said.

"I don't know, I... I think so."

Jai'Lune whipped her phone out. "I'm gonna get online and see what people are saying."

They plopped down on the couch and Eva stared over Jai'Lune's shoulder, watching her scroll. "Look! This is crazy! People are saying it was an earthquake. Nebraska doesn't get earthquakes!"

"Oh my gosh, it was just a tiny rumbling. Look." She held the phone up and Eva could see. Both coasts had suffered massive earthquakes at the same time. Jai'Lune kept scrolling. "People are saying the plates are doing some crazy shifting under the earth."

Eva rubbed her sweaty palms on her jeans and began going around the house, shoving books back on shelves and checking for damage. If that was just rumblings, she would hate to know what the real thing felt like.

"Oh my gosh, people are panicking. They say a wave is about to hit the coasts. They have to get out of there."

Eva's stomach dropped at the thought. She realized she should let Gramps, Gram, and Mom know she was okay. She found her phone and sent a quick text to them. Someone knocked on the door. In all the chaos, she had forgotten about her date, but like clockwork, Alex had shown up at her door. She opened the door with a nervous smile and let him in. A wave of relief washed over her at the sight of him. Somehow, with Alex there, she felt safer. *Why?* She shook her head; she was fine on her own. She always had been.

Chapter Twenty-Three

"Did you guys feel that?" Alex asked Jai'Lune and Eva.

"Hard to miss. Jai'Lune felt it too." Eva lifted her eyebrows, hoping he got her point. *It must have been real, not spiritual.*

"How on earth could I miss it?" Jai'Lune stared at them as if they were both insane. "They're worried about aftershocks and giant waves on the coasts."

"Giant waves?" Alex asked. *Like the dreams.* Were the dreams coming true? Alex's stomach turned at the thought. Eva's expression reflected the terror he was feeling.

"For the first time in my life, I'm glad we live in Nebraska. We're furthest from both oceans," Jai'Lune said.

"Agreed! We better get going, Alex. I don't want to be late for Ellie's." As they headed for the door, Alex saw Eva exchange a glance with Jai'Lune. What did it mean? He wasn't sure, but he hoped it didn't mean she was dreading this. He'd been excited and nervous about it all day, but now that it was here, he was losing a little confidence.

"You kids have fun!" Jai'Lune waved, walking out behind them. "I'm headed to the Tasteez to get the lowdown." She did some goofy little dance move that made Alex laugh. He didn't know what it was about Jai'Lune, but he instinctively liked her.

It was dark outside as they pulled up to Ellie's Cafe. The parking lot was empty, but the café lights were on. Eva could see Grace inside, wiping off tables. When they knocked on the glass door, it startled her. Recognition dawned on her face, and she let them in. The smell of homemade pie washed over Alex, and his stomach growled. He hadn't realized how hungry he was. He'd been too nervous to eat most of the day.

"How's it going?" Eva asked.

"Not too bad. Ellie's in the back. I told her we had something bothering us, and we were hoping she could help. That's all she knows."

Eva nodded. Ellie came out of the back, wiping her hands on a white towel. "Well, look what the cat dragged in! How are you two? Eva, you a little better than the last time I saw you. Been drinking your water?"

"Yes ma'am, I've been trying."

"That's a good girl. Keep up the good work."

"Thanks?" Eva said, blushing. Alex smirked. Ellie was always mothering everyone. She had a way about her. She took charge of any room she entered, and somehow you knew, when Ellie was in charge, everything was going to be okay.

Ellie turned to Alex. "And you, sir. That touchdown pass last night." She whistled. "WowWee, that was something to behold. We ain't had a player like you at Marysburg High since Eva's dad was here."

Alex hadn't realized Russell was an athlete. Nice, an easy topic to bring up next time. "You know, as an athlete, you gotta treat your body like a machine. Take good care of it. Water is the oil that keeps everything running smooth. Your coaches been telling you that? Water flushes out all the gunk in those big muscles 'a yours."

Now it was Alex's turn to be embarrassed. "Yes, Miss Ellie. They tell us to stay hydrated. I try to."

"Well, that's a good boy. Why don't you two help Grace wipe down the rest of the tables?" She handed them well-worn rags that were identical to Grace's. While they worked, Ellie kept up the conversation. "Where do you work now, Eva? At the Care Center?"

"Yep, evenings and weekends in the kitchen."

"Well, I'm always in need of good help. You ever get sick 'a those old people, you trade 'em in for a younger model and come work for me. I'm no spring chicken, but I got at least twenty years on those old folks." She laughed, which made Alex and Eva laugh.

"I'm serious though, honey. You ever need a job, don't be afraid to ask, understand? You too, Alex. Though I don't suppose you have much time leftover with all those sports." He smiled. A part of him would love to work for her.

"Thanks, Ellie," Eva said with a smile.

"You bet, sweetheart. It's the least I can do. Your daddy was a good worker for me back when he was in school, before his no-good momma—God rest her soul—shipped him off, that is. I woulda taken him home with me if I could. He was a good kid, your daddy. A hard worker," Ellie rambled on. "Shy, though. Always real quiet and serious. Your momma and him were cute as a button together. Those were tough times back then, tough times..." She trailed off for a second, as if lost in her own thoughts. Then she said, "Oh, but I shouldn't be lamenting the past. If the good Lord intended us to move backward, he woulda made time work that way."

Grace took their rags in a bucket to the sink, then she said to Ellie, "The past is kind of what we wanted to talk to you about. Do you remember what was going on way back then with Eva's dad?"

"Now, why you asking me that? You children don't be

going an' stirring up trouble for yourself." She pointed at Alex. "You need to mind your p's and q's. Don't go risking those football scholarships, you hear?" Alex nodded, but he wasn't sure how much he cared about the scholarships or how this could affect them anyhow.

"Why don't you kids sit down here and tell me what's going on?" She gestured to a corner booth.

They settled in and Grace began. "You know about what happened when Eva's parents were in school."

"Well sure. Biggest mess I ever saw, what happened back then. Those kids going on about some dreams, and all the adults calling them possessed. Nonsense, if you ask me."

Alex glanced at Eva. Had they made a mistake coming to Ellie if she thought the dreams were crazy? Eva didn't notice, or at least didn't acknowledge, his glance, and he turned his attention back to Ellie. She was down-to-earth, and it was one thing people loved about her. It made her trustworthy. When she said something, people listened. But would she be too down-to-earth to believe them?

Grace took a deep breath and barreled on. "Some of us are having the same dreams they had back then. We didn't know anything about it until the dreams began. Now we're searching for answers, trying to figure out what to do next."

"Hmm. And you all are having them?" Ellie stared at each of them as they nodded. "What happens in these dreams 'a yours?"

"There's always these three black tornados," Grace answered. "We try to warn people, but no one will listen."

"Uh-huh, I see. *Three* black tornados you say, not two?" They nodded.

"We've been talking to Eva's dad," Grace admitted. "And we also found out online that kids all over the world are having the dreams too."

"Really?" Ellie's eyes grew wide, and her mouth opened in surprise.

Eva piped up, "Russell thinks things are happening faster and maybe it's culminating or something."

"What exactly is culminating, honey?"

Eva stared down at the table. Was she embarrassed? "He thinks some evil is coming and we need to warn people."

Ellie crossed herself and whispered the name of Jesus three times. "What's this got to do with me, children?"

"We don't know. But Eva's dad told her and me to pray for someone to help. The next thing we knew, Grace was suggesting you. We had to try," Alex said. He wondered if their desperation was as obvious as it felt.

"Everyone in town thinks Russell is crazy. No one's gonna listen to him, but they'll listen to you," Eva said.

"Everyone sees you as the town mom," Grace said to Ellie. "We thought if you believed us, maybe you could help us talk to other people, too."

Ellie chuckled at that. "Town mom, huh? Is that any relation to Father Time?" She laughed at her own joke, squinted one eye and got serious. "You think the dreams mean some sorta darkness is coming and we need to warn people? What we need to warn them about?"

"My Great Granny thinks we need to warn them to pray. She says the dreams are a warning and whatever they're warning us about is gonna happen soon cause our dreams have three tornados and that's a sign of completion."

At that, Ellie snapped to attention. "You talked to your Great Granny Maggie about this? What else did she say?"

"Nothing much. She mostly listened. Why?"

"I don't want to get wrapped up in all this. And maybe I shouldn't be telling you this now." Ellie hesitated before continuing. "But I been having those same dreams since long before your parents were born."

They all sat stunned, staring at Ellie. Then Grace blurted, "You have?"

"Yep. You get used to them the way you get used to an ache in your back, and they don't take over your life anymore. But I was confused when it went from two tornados to three a few months ago. I betcha Maggie's right, the times coming sooner than we thought."

"I can't believe Great Granny Maggie didn't tell me you had the dreams too."

"Course she didn't tell you. She was sworn to secrecy by yours truly!"

"Are there other people like you, adults, who have the dreams still?" Alex asked.

"Well, now, you'd have to talk to Maggie about that," she said with a knowing gleam in her eye. "We adults have a lot to lose if we go running our mouths. I have the café to think about. Folks think I'm crazy, they not coming in here for pie, you see? All those years ago, it was even more of a risk. I was a single mom in a small town with two kids to raise. I couldn't afford to lose business over a few dreams. When I think back on it now, well, maybe I shoulda said something to help those kids out."

"Does that mean you'll help us?" Grace asked.

"Help you with what?"

"I don't know. Help us warn people to pray, I guess. Or help us know what on earth to do next," Grace said.

"Honey, you had the dreams, right? You know people gonna ignore us even if we shout it from the rooftops."

"But we have to *try*, don't we?" Grace asked. "You said it yourself that you shoulda helped those kids years ago. You can't change the past, but you could help change the future." Alex thought it was a compelling argument, but would Ellie agree? She was silently tilting her head side to side as if debating with herself.

Finally, she spoke. "I do got less to lose these days. I'm getting almost too old to run this place, anyway." She heaved a deep sigh. "Maybe this is my golden opportunity to right some wrongs I done in the past before these old bones give up the ghost. Okay children, I'll help you."

Alex and Eva smiled. Grace let out a little squeal of excitement. "Okay, what should we do next?"

"Well, now, how should I know? I got brought in on all this nonsense two seconds ago!"

"Come on, Ellie," Eva urged. "After all these years, you must have a plan. Something you imagined yourself doing."

Ellie grinned at Eva. "You know how I always thought about doing it? Putting an anonymous letter in the Marysburg Newspaper. Everybody in town still gets that old newspaper, either online or in the mail. It'd be the perfect way to get the word out without bringing down the wrath of this small town on us. Maybe it's an okay idea to try."

"But what if they figure out who we are?" Grace fidgeted with her hands and readjusted in her seat, as if realizing for the first time what this could cost her.

"Stan, down at the paper, owes me a favor. He'll keep our identities secret, no matter who asks. We were high school sweethearts, you know." She winked and pressed her lips together in a smile. "But he went off to the war, and I got married to that no-good husband of mine, God rest his soul."

She waved her hands to dismiss the topic. "Water under the bridge. Yes, you write the note and I'll deliver it. After a bit, if they don't listen, we can write another. If we can motivate them to get praying, that should help. Don't you think?"

"It's a start," Alex admitted.

"That it is. We'll see where the good Lord takes us from there. Grace, if you see your Great Granny Maggie, you tell her I let the cat outta the bag about me having the dreams. Will ya?"

"You bet." Grace nodded.

"Now, if you don't mind, it's time for me to get some rest."

They stood up. "Thanks for your help, Ellie," Eva said.

Ellie hauled her considerable weight up out of the seat. "Well, now, it's nothing I shouldn't a done for your daddy a long time ago. If you see him, you tell him Ellie says hi, and he oughta stop in for a piece of pie some time. Ask him if lemon meringue's still his favorite."

"Okay," Eva said with a smile.

"Oh Grace, be a dear and grab their to go bags outta the warmer for me, would ya?" Alex had almost forgotten about his date with Eva. His stomach bunched up in knots again.

"You kids have a good night, now," Ellie said as they stepped out the front door. She locked the door behind them and turned to go to her apartment above the café.

In the gravel parking lot, Grace said, "I think that went well. How about you guys?"

"I think so," Eva said. "At least we have our next step."

Chapter Twenty-Four

As Grace walked away, Alex turned to Eva. "Shall we?"

"We shall."

They walked to his pickup, and a mixture of nerves and excitement bubbled up in Alex's blood. "I thought maybe we could eat and talk by the creek on S curve road."

"Okay," was all she said.

Did she think it was stupid? "We could go somewhere else too. The park maybe?"

"No," she said, and gave him a smile. "I like your idea."

"Okay." They rode in silence as he guided his truck onto the gravel S curve road that earned its nickname because of all the twists and turns. It mirrored the bends in the creek and took all Alex's attention, but the truck seemed too quiet. *Say something, you weirdo.* But he didn't know what to say. "Uh, want some music? You can turn on whatever you want."

"Sure," she said and leaned forward to flip on the radio. She scrolled through until she found a station playing 90s country and sat back.

"You like this old stuff, too?"

"I listened to it with Gramps when I was little. I guess it kinda stuck."

"Same. Pops loves it, so it's on a loop whenever we drive."

"How'd you know about the spot on S curve road?" she asked, sounding suspicious.

"Pops and I found it a few years back when we were fishing. I always wanted to bring... well, I mean, it's nice, you'll see." What he didn't say is that he'd always thought someday he'd bring someone special here to share it with them. Funny, it never crossed his mind to bring Janet when they were together. But with Eva, it was the first thing he thought of.

Alex turned off the road onto a path between two cornfields. Soon his headlights were illuminating the creek bank with tree branches hanging low on both sides. The leaves glowed burnt orange in the light from his headlights, but a thick backdrop of darkness surrounded them. A deer was drinking from the creek. It lifted its head, startled from the noise, and stood frozen for a moment. Then it ran off into the trees.

"Pretty," Eva said with a sigh. He smiled. Somehow, he knew she'd enjoy it.

She opened the bag of food from Ellie's and his stomach growled loudly. "Sorry," he said, embarrassed.

She laughed it off, and it made his nerves settle a bit. "I wasn't sure what you'd want, so I went with the classics—hamburgers, fries, and chocolate shakes. Hope that's okay."

"It's perfect," Alex assured her, unwrapping a burger. The radio played *Meet in the Middle* in the background as he searched for something to say. "Did you really have fun at the football game, or were you just saying that?"

She pushed her lips together and nodded her head. He wondered what she was thinking, but he didn't have to wonder for long. She said what she was thinking. "I like how you cut to the chase. Small talk drives me nuts."

"Same. I thought all girls liked small talk. They're always talking so much."

She dropped her head and peered at him through squinted eyes. "I'm not most girls."

"You most definitely are not."

Her face got a little red, but she pushed through. "To answer your question, I'm kinda surprised how much fun I had last night. I never understood why people got into football, but I think it might have something to do with the atmosphere. The crowd was electric. How about you? Why do you like it?"

"I don't know. It's an adrenaline rush, I guess. You get out there and you're nervous, but then your body clicks, and you get into the zone, you know?"

"I most definitely do not know, never been an athlete. I'd be terrified to do anything in front of a big crowd."

"It's not something I want to do forever."

"Because you want to be a vet?"

"You remembered." That must be a good sign if she cared enough to remember the details. *Maybe she did like him, just a little.*

"Of course! I'm a big animal fan too."

"That's cool. Pops and I are trying to tame a wild coon. You should come see the little fuzzball sometime. I saw you had a dog."

"Yeah, Flip. He's great. My little sidekick when mom's at work every night."

"Yeah, dogs are great company. Your mom works a lot?" *Was he prying?*

"Only constantly." She shrugged.

"I bet that can get lonely." He knew a thing or two about being alone. Maybe she did too.

Their food was gone, the empty wrappers shoved back in the bag. "Want to go check out the creek?"

She nodded, "Okay. I just hope we don't find any more black gateways of death."

He laughed. "Is that what we're calling them now?"

"I don't know, but that was creepy." *He had to agree.*

The cows had worn a path through the grass down to the creek and they followed it with Alex walking in front. As they walked, Eva said, "You know, I really don't get it."

Alex sensed frustration in her voice, and he turned to glance at her. "What?"

"I've known you my whole life, and you barely acknowledged my existence. But all the sudden this school year we're eating burgers in your truck and talking about life as if it's all perfectly normal."

He couldn't explain it to her, and he was nervous about what to say next. He glanced at her like the deer they'd startled by the creek. For a moment, he wanted to follow its example and flee into the field. But he stood his ground and told her the truth. "I honestly don't know, Eva. Ever since the dreams and stuff, I'm drawn to you like a magnet. It's like something inside of me is attracted to something inside of you." The heat of embarrassment made its way up his cheeks as he waited for her response.

"Well, that's... weirdly sweet," Eva said, and he let out the breath he didn't know he'd been holding. "You're full of surprises Alex Smith. Full of surprises."

After they walked for a bit, she asked, "Who do you hang out with? You probably have all kinds of friends, but who's your best friend?"

"I don't have a lot of friends." He hated to admit it, but it was true.

"You're the quarterback of the football team. The hometown legend. The town worships you. What do you mean, you don't have many friends?"

"I might have fans, but I don't have friends."

"You have the entire team," she pointed out.

"But we don't hang out. After football they go their way and I go mine. They don't... invite me. It's just when we're at school we're together." Great, now he was telling her his whole loser life story. Not how he pictured the evening going. He shrugged in the dark. "I'm shy. It's tough. Social cues. They get me every time."

"I get that."

"You do?"

"Sure! You don't see me battling crowds of friends drawn to my sparkling personality, do you? It's me and Jai'Lune. That's how it's always been."

"Sure would be nice to have someone to hang out with," he admitted. "She's pretty cool."

"She is." Eva paused for a moment. "I suppose all this craziness doesn't make it any easier for you to make friends. It's hard to act normal when you see shadows no one else can see."

"Basically. It's nice to be with someone who gets that."

"Have you told anyone else you're having the dreams?"

"The guys online. And you and Grace."

"How about your parents? Think you'll tell them?"

He cleared his throat. "Every time I try to tell my mom, I can't spit the words out. It's bizarre, you know? If what Russell said is true, then one or both of my parents probably had the dreams when they were my age. They might understand, but..."

"Why didn't they warn you about them?"

"Exactly." *Man, it was good to be understood.*

"Are you close with your parents?" Eva asked.

"Mom and I are close. Dad can be moody and dark sometimes. He's intense. I try not to push his buttons. That's the extent of our relationship. Not that great, I guess. You? Close with your mom?"

"I respect her, but I wouldn't say we're close. She's not around that much, you know? She works all the time and when she's around, it still feels like she's somewhere else. But I know she tries hard. I feel bad wishing she was different."

"I know what you mean," he said, thinking about his dad.

Chapter Twenty-Five

Sitting beside Alex on the way back to her house, she had to admit she'd pegged him all wrong. The jock factor threw her off, and she had all these preconceived notions about him that weren't true. Or fair. One by one he'd broken them all down. Underneath, she was surprised to discover a depth she never expected.

His shyness was the first thing that shocked her. How could she have never realized he was as shy and awkward as her? *I guess we all have more to our story than meets the eye.* Alex dropped Eva off at home and she hoped he wouldn't try to kiss her. *Too soon, buddy, I'd have to punch you.* She was relieved when he just smiled. "I had a nice time with you, Eva. I really like hanging out with you."

She was only slightly reluctant to admit she felt the same. "Thanks, it was fun." Eva hopped out of the car and had a little bounce in her step as she walked to the door and shut it firmly behind her.

All the lights in her living room flipped on, momentarily blinding her. "What do you think you're doing, young lady?" Her mom's voice said from somewhere in the room.

Eva flinched, shielding her eyes with a hand, "Wha... what?"

"What do you think gives you the right, Eva Marie Thompson?" Eva peeked out from under her hand. Her mom's cheeks were flushed, and she had fire in her eyes. Was she mad about Eva going out with Alex? She didn't understand why that would upset her.

The color drained from Eva's face. Russell. She knew.

"I did everything to protect you from him. I worked two jobs and raised you all on my own. Now he slinks back into town, thinking he can play dad. I don't think so. I forbid you from seeing him, Eva. I forbid it!"

She was running her hands through her hair and pacing back and forth, but she stopped every once in a while to point her finger at Eva. She'd never seen her mom this passionate about anything.

"That gossipy old hag comes in the store and tells me he's back in town. That's bad enough. Then she says your car's been over there. I can't believe you... you know what? No. He's the adult in this situation. I'm going over there. I'm going to give him a piece of my mind once and for all. He has no right to be here. I told him never to come back."

She stormed out of the house and Eva stared after her, blinking. A second later, Eva bolted out the door after her. "Mom, no. Please."

Her mom shoved Eva's hand off her arm and got in her car. Eva grabbed her phone from her pocket and texted Russell, 'Mom's coming to see you. She found out you moved back, and I went to see you. She's mad. Sorry.'

A few seconds later, her phone buzzed. 'No problem. Thanks for telling me.'

~

Eva sat on the couch, tapping her foot on the floor. She got up and paced. Flip followed her. She couldn't stay here waiting. Eva grabbed her keys and headed to Jai'Lune's house.

"Eva, it's late, what are you doing?" Jai'Lune said through a yawn as Eva barged into her bedroom.

"She knows."

"What?"

"Mom knows I've been hanging out with Russell, and she's mad. She went over there."

"She went over where? Your dad's?" Jai'Lune asked, stretching.

"Yes! She's there right now, and I'm freaking out."

"Okay, calm down. We can handle this. We can handle this." But her face said, *we can't handle this.*

"I know! What am I going to do? Is she going to kick him out of town again?"

"She can't do that, Eva. He's an adult."

"I know, but she kept him out of my life for this long. What if she does it again? You know what? No. I will not let her. He's *my* father, and I have a right to have him in my life if I want. I'm going over there."

"You're what? No, you aren't!" She threw her blankets off, awake now.

"Yes, I am. I'm going over there right now, and I'm going to tell mom she better lay off, because he's *my* father, and I want him in my life."

"Do you, Eva? Do you want him in your life?" Eva hadn't realized until that moment, when she thought she might lose him again, how much she wanted Russell in her life. Close to tears, all she could do was nod her head yes.

"I'll get my coat. I'm going with you."

Jai'Lune drove, and Eva fumed in the passenger seat. "I mean, seriously, what gives her the right?"

Jai'Lune was driving slow for the first time in her life, as they turned onto Russell's road. "What are you doing? Hurry!"

"I'm giving you a chance to calm down! Geez, Eva, I've never seen you this way." Jai'Lune didn't know how it felt to live your whole life without a father. Then, right when he came back to town, to have someone try to take him away again. Or maybe she did, Eva realized, wincing as she remembered Jai'Lune was adopted. Russell's house came into view and she took a deep breath.

"Kill the lights."

"What?"

"Turn your lights off. I don't want them to see we're here."

"Finally, you're coming to your senses."

"No, I want to see what's happening first."

Jai'Lune grimaced but shut off her lights before turning onto Russell's long lane, going slower than ever now. The porch light was on, and in the small halo of light, Eva could see her mom, red-faced and yelling. Russell stood there, attentive but neutral. When her mom stopped to take a breath, or sob, she couldn't tell which, he embraced her in a hug.

At first, her mom tried to push him away, but he was saying something to her. Then he was stroking her hair, and for a moment Eva almost thought they were going to kiss. Gross! "Okay, let's go."

Jai'Lune flipped on the lights and stepped on the gas, propelling them down the rest of the lane. Eva's parents turned in surprise. She jumped out of the car, almost before Jai'Lune came to a complete stop. "Eva, what are you doing here?" Her mom asked.

"I'm not letting you kick him out of my life again, Mom," Eva yelled. "He's a good guy. It's about time you saw that. He's not a drunk teenager anymore."

Was that a grin on Russell's face? Eva's mom glared at him, and he held up his hands in an 'it's true' gesture. To Eva's great astonishment, her mom burst into a loud laugh. "Eva, you're as crazy as he is!"

Eva didn't know what to say to that and Russell apparently didn't either. They both stood there like idiots, waiting for her next words. Her mom glanced back and forth from Eva's face to Russell's several times. With a sigh, she said, "I suppose maybe Eva is old enough to make her own choices. If she wants you in her life, I can't stop her." She stalked down the porch steps, walked right past Eva, and slammed the car door behind her.

After she drove away, Eva glanced at Russell. "What did you say to her? I thought she was going to tear you to shreds, but she just... gave in."

"I said I was sorry. It's my fault I ripped apart this family, and there's not a day goes by I don't pray God will put us all back together. I can't change the past. All I could say was sorry. And that I still love her. Love you. And I'd die before I ever did anything to hurt either of you again."

His words stunned Eva. To think he still loved her mom after all these years. After all she'd done to him. Kept him from. And to think her own father might love her. It was a concept she couldn't wrap her mind around yet.

Eva walked back to the car where Jai'Lune sat, wide-eyed and gripping the steering wheel. They drove away, Russell still standing in the pale white glow of the porch light.

Chapter Twenty-Six

Alex's mind was still buzzing from his date with Eva when he got home. He kept going over everything he'd said, they'd said. The more he got to know her, the more he liked her. She was right. He'd never noticed her until this school year. How could he have been this blind? She was standing right in front of him the whole time.

Alex went to bed and tried to read his book, but his mind was still racing. He wouldn't be getting to sleep anytime soon. The stack of his dad's journals Pops gave him sat on his desk in the corner, unopened. Maybe he should read them? The memory of the day Pops gave them to him came rushing back. Alex's dad had just chewed him out. Again. This time in front of Pops. Alex was down about it but trying not to show it.

Pops had an air of sad nostalgia about him that day when he gave Alex his father's journals. "I maybe shouldn't be doing this. I don't typically stick my nose in other people's business. But I know your dad is hard on you. I was hard on him, too. Probably too hard. Things look different when you look back."

He handed Alex a giant stack of dusty spiral bound notebooks. "I found these in the attic. Read them sometime. It might give you a glimpse at who your dad was before he joined the service. Who I was back then, too. Maybe it'll help you go easy on him when he gets all outta hand."

But Alex was too mad to be interested in his dad's old journals. He set them on his desk and forgot about them. Now the sight of them made him curious, especially if his dad had the dreams back then. Alex grabbed the top journal and flipped to a random page.

September 19, 2001. I've been having some weird dreams. There are these two black tornados. I mean, they're blacker than night, and they're ripping through the sky. I'm screaming like a maniac, telling everybody to take cover, but they all ignore me. It's frustrating. I hope they stop soon.

Alex froze. *It was his dad who had the dreams.* This whole time, he had been assuming it was his mom. Dad was too narrow-minded to have the dreams. Alex couldn't imagine he'd ever believe something this bizarre was real.

September 23, 2001. Today after church I was wandering around, waiting for Mom to finish talking, and I discovered the church library. It was full of dusty, old books, but this one book was calling my name. So, I brought it home. It's interesting. It talks about what a significant advantage we have because we can pray. I never thought of praying as an advantage. More like a boring obligation at church.

It said we all have a guardian angel, too. Apparently, everyone gets one at birth, and the angel's only job is to protect us and help us get back to heaven. It's weird to think there's an angel in my room.

Apparently, we can ask God to super-charge our guardian angel to give them more power to protect us. Do they get all buff and stuff? I want mine to be ripped. Maybe I'll try it. Every day before weights, I could do a little spiritual weightlifting for my angel dude. Here's the prayer the book had, so I don't forget it:

Angel of God, my Guardian dear, to whom God's love commits me here, ever this day be at my side, to light, to guard, to rule, to guide. Amen.

Alex wondered if his dad kept up the prayer or if he forgot about it. There was a month's gap before the next entry.

October 31, 2001. I'm still having those weird dreams. They're getting annoying. Speaking of annoying, Carol and I went to that creepy valley on the property next to ours. My dad always told me to keep my distance, but she said we should check it out since it's Halloween time and all that. She thought it'd be fun.

I didn't want to go, but she wouldn't give it up. I didn't want her to go alone, so I went with her. We both kinda freaked out when we got there. That's some nasty something down there. We couldn't get close to it, whatever it is, but a million miles away is too close if you ask me. Something doesn't feel right about that place.

November 12, 2001. I can't believe it. Carol's having the same dreams as me. She's all wigged out about it. And now weird stuff is happening to me when I'm awake. I hear my voice in my head, but it's saying nasty things. Horrible stuff.

It's confusing because it sounds like me, but it's not me thinking it. I'm hearing it. Like it said, my mom hates me and everyone's out to get me. I know Mom doesn't hate me. But the voices are tricky. Sometimes I almost believe them. It's like I'm drowning, and I can't remember which way is up. I told my dad about it, but he told me to keep my mouth shut, or people would think I'm crazy… maybe I am crazy.

Alex couldn't believe it. *Both* his parents were having the dreams when they were his age? Why hadn't they ever mentioned it? Maybe he should have told them he was having them. What if they knew how to help? He read on.

November 16, 2001. Carol and I found out Russell Thompson, Rachel Tooley, and Spencer O'Donnell are having the dreams too. It's freaking us all out. We all think they're some kind of warning, but we have no clue what they're trying to warn us about.

When we try to tell the adults, they're like the people in our dreams, none of them listen. They tell us to ignore the dreams and they'll go away, as if they know. How could we ever ignore them?

History was repeating itself. First in Alex's dad's generation and now in his. Alex wondered how many people in his small town knew about the dreams. Did it actually go as far back as the first settlers? He shivered and picked up another notebook dated five years later.

January 19, 2006. The nights are the worst. I'm fine when I'm with someone, but as soon as I'm alone, the voices and attack begin. The fear is the worst, though. It pushes in on me until it's like it becomes me or something.

The evil makes itself look like whatever I'm fearing most. Sometimes it's something beautiful, like Carol, but suddenly it explodes into this horrible beast.

I met this guy named Father Thomas. He told me Satan used to be an angel, and angels can change forms to do God's will. Even though Satan is a fallen angel and only serves himself, he can still change forms. It freaked me out, but maybe it explains a lot about what I'm experiencing.

The attacks sound even worse for his father than they were for Alex. *Was it going to get worse?* Dread poured into his veins.

February 2, 2006. Last night I was lying in bed with my book light on, trying to read, when I had this immense feeling of dread. It was evil, and I could sense it creeping closer and closer. I prayed the way Father Thomas taught me. "God, don't let the fear take over. Give me strength to hold on to you." I could sense the evil seeping in like an evening mist. Over and over, I said out loud, "My God is stronger than you.

My God is stronger than you." But the evil said, "No, He's not."

I did my best to keep my voice calm. "Yes, He is!" We kept going back and forth as it crept closer. Just as it looked ready to pounce, my book light got radiant, and a voice said, "Yes, I am. I Am Who I Am, and you will harm him no longer." It was as if I could hear the voice with my ears, but I knew it was coming from my heart.

The evil instantly shrank back and got small, cowering outside my bedroom door. When the voice stopped speaking, the evil got angry and tried to attack even harder, but God wouldn't let it. It couldn't even come through the door. It's like I was witnessing a spiritual battle or something.

Russell had talked about a spiritual battle. Turns out his dad had figured it out, too. Maybe that's why he drilled them about battle so much. It was his twisted way of making sure they were ready for this. Alex read the next entry from a few weeks later.

February 20, 2006. I told Father Thomas what happened. He explained to me a little about how the spiritual world works. He said the spiritual world has a stream of white light, crackling with electricity. With our prayer, we can plug into that power. We can soak up the power ourselves, and we're stronger in the spiritual sense.

Father Thomas said when we pray, our light gets brighter and brighter in the spiritual world because we're tapping into the power of God. We're more protected from the evil. We can pray for our guardian angel, and it does the same for them.

I never used to pray before. I mean, not much. Father Thomas said when we don't pray and tap into that spiritual power, we walk around empty. When we're empty, we're more vulnerable to the evil attacks. We're weak and spiritually defenseless, and the evil has an easy win.

It doesn't play fair either. It kicks us in places we're already hurting or vulnerable, like if we break up with someone, it will convince us that the person never loved us and we're unlovable. Or if we don't like something about ourselves, it will try to convince us it's way worse than it is. It'll poke us in the wound. That's why a lot of times we are hopeless and sad. We don't even realize what's going on. That invisible forces are trying to break us down. Father Thomas said he could teach me to pray and tap into the spiritual power.

Alex glanced around his room, processing what he'd read. His eyes rested on the long, skinny dresser to the left with the pale wood he'd always thought was ugly. Then they drifted to the window where the moonlight was streaming in, highlighting his mismatched tall dresser to the right. Such ordinary things surrounded him as he tried to comprehend something so extraordinary.

March 15, 2006. I've been praying like a crazy fool and the attacks are better. Now I just wish I could get the tornado dreams out of my head. They're unfinished business. I wish I knew what they symbolized. Father Thomas said to ask God to help me understand. Maybe I should tell people to pray, or show them how, since it helped me so much, but I don't want to. It's weird, and how would I do it anyhow?

I get frustrated when Father Thomas won't give me answers. It's annoying. He always tells me to pray about it. But what else can I do? I've been trying. The darkness is ramping up. It's like the evil is a bunch of military troops. I wish I knew some military tactics so I could defend myself.

Was that why his dad joined the military, to learn more about it? But why didn't he ever say anything to Alex about it? He'd shown them plenty of military tactics growing up, but never mentioned the spiritual stuff. It would have been helpful if he did. Maybe he thought Alex wouldn't understand. Maybe he was right.

May 8, 2006. I joined the Army today. The evil has been

trying to stop my research in all kinds of nasty ways. First, I got super sick. Then I had a flat tire. Just when I got that paid off, my apartment sprung a leak and ruined half my stuff, but I've been praying every day the way Father Thomas taught me. I'm stronger now.

I have this sense God is saying the Army is the way to go for me. Guess I'll give it a try. It can't hurt and I need the money, anyway. Maybe I'll learn some tactics to help me fight the evil. When I have kids, I'm gonna show them how to defend themselves so they can be strong. I'm such a wimp half the time.

Is that what Pops wanted Alex to see? Was his dad hard on him because he was trying to protect him? When was he going to teach Alex the spiritual stuff? Because Alex needed *that* kind of help right now. *Maybe he could talk to his dad.* How would he even bring up this stuff, though? As he was thinking about it, Alex drifted into a fitful sleep.

Alex could feel the metal of the seat beneath him. Ax marks were visible on the rough-hewn floor from where they'd chopped down the trees to make the schoolhouse. A pot-belly stove gave off heat as the teacher droned on, and the old-fashioned chalkboard was covered in writing.

Through the window beside his desk, Alex saw the sky growing dark. As he watched, the clouds churned before his eyes, and three tornados formed fingers of death. Alex screamed and turned back to the classroom. "The tornados are coming!"

"That is quite enough, young man." The teacher walked toward him with a paddle in her hand. "I'll not have you disrupting my classroom." The other students sat staring straight ahead, as if nothing was happening.

"But it's... see for yourself." Alex pointed out the window.

"I will do no such thing." The flesh of her face melted as if she was decaying right in front of him. "My students are quite happy learning what they are. We don't need you coming in here, stirring the pot."

Alex slid out of his seat and shoved the schoolhouse door open with a bang. The sunshine hit his face, and he woke up.

Chapter Twenty-Seven

The light was streaming in through Eva's window. She rolled over on her side and stared at Flip, asleep on her rug. She was close to falling back asleep when she heard a thought. "Write." Eva covered her head with her pillow. *Was this another weird spiritual experience?* She wasn't in the mood.

"Write," the voice said again, the volume unaffected by the pillow.

"No," Eva whined to the empty room like an insane person. "I'm tired."

"Write," Eva heard again, persistent but not forceful.

"I don't have anything to say." Eva pulled the covers over her head.

"Listen and write."

Eva threw the covers off. "Fine! Then I'm going back to sleep." This was not her idea of a Sunday morning. *Or maybe it was another dream?* She wondered. With a grumpy flop, she sat up in bed and grabbed her notebook and a pen from the nightstand. The moment she opened it, words started coming to her, and she wrote.

It was slow going at first, each word coming to her, repeating until she wrote it. Then the next word would come. Eva thought to the imaginary voice, "You must be new at this." She heard a faint chuckle, but the words kept coming. She was listening with such intensity that she didn't realize what she'd written until it was done, and she went back to read it.

To whom it may concern:

There is a lot going on in our world we cannot explain. Sickness and violence and slaughter. But to each thing, there is a tie back to a failure.

What is this failure? I cannot say for you, but for me, it is the failure to connect with a God who loves me. A failure to understand that a relationship with Him would make my life better, not worse. A relationship built on true mutual respect instead of rules and condemnation.

The universe is in God's hands. When we live according to universal law, our lives are better. Anyone who chooses otherwise risks paying gravely for their decision.

I urge you, brothers and sisters, to seek a relationship with God. Listen to God calling your heart deep within and answer that call. Go to church. Say a prayer. Read your Bible. Do what you need to in order to foster a relationship with the one who made you, because a time is coming when you'll wish you had.

The darkness is coming soon—a blackness this town has never seen. When it does, all hell will rain down. If you're not protected, you'll be wiped out. Time is running out to make the right choice.

Eva leaned back on her pillow and let out the breath she didn't realize she was holding. She was a good writer, but this had words in it she didn't even know. What was universal law? And *what* had just happened to her?

Eva heard another extremely different voice, low and quiet as the hiss of a snake. She strained the muscles of her mind to hear it. "You always ruin everything, Eva. You are the worst thing God has ever created, and he wishes you were dead."

Eva shook her head, but the voice got louder, "God is angry at you—at everybody—and He's coming to destroy all of you. You're all going to die, and God is going to kill you, because you are worthless and stupid. It's why your father left you. It's why your mom is never around. They all want to get away from *you*."

"No!" Eva said, throwing back the covers and standing up. "No, you're wrong." This was an attack, and she knew it. She just didn't know how to stop it.

"I'm right, and you know it. That's why it upsets you this much. You know, somewhere deep inside, you are evil. You're afraid people will find out how worthless you are. You hide, Eva, but I know your secret and they do too. It's obvious to everyone. You can't hide from it any longer."

Eva clutched her head with her hands. She wanted to make the voice stop. How could she make it stop? She remembered Alex saying, "Jesus, help me," when the dog attacked. When he said it, it was as if a blindfold was removed from her eyes. In a loud voice, she said, "Jesus, help me." She said it again and again, then shouted it. "Jesus, help!"

The voice in Eva's head went silent, as if ripped from her ears. Whatever had been there a moment ago was gone. She sat down on the edge of her bed, exhausted. *What was that?*

The bottle of holy water hummed on her dresser where she'd left it. Eva picked it up and unscrewed the lid. She walked around her room, splashing water out of the bottle and saying, "I bless this house in the name of Jesus Christ."

It might be crazy, but at this point, she'd try whatever she could to make the evil go away. When she was done with her room, she didn't stop there. She went on to the next room and the next, splashing the holy water and saying over and over, "I bless this house in the name of Jesus Christ." Each time she flicked water, she remembered a time when she was scared, and her voice grew stronger. "I bless this house in the name of Jesus Christ. I bless this house in the name of Jesus Christ. I bless this house in the name of Jesus Christ."

The evil had attacked Eva in her own bedroom, in her own home, but it would not happen again. She was mad, and she was taking back her territory. She picked up her phone and touched a name. The phone rang and someone picked up. "Gram?"

"Yes, honey, what is it? Is something wrong?" Eva realized what time it was.

"Sorry to call this early. I wondered if I could go to church with you today?" The silence rang loud. Maybe the call had dropped. "Gram?"

"Yes, honey, sorry I'm still here. Of course, you can go to church with us. We'll pick you up a little before nine."

"Okay, see you then." Eva was about to hang up when the thought struck her. "What should I wear?"

"Wear whatever you want! Hallelujah, you're going to church!" Her voice sounded like she was dancing a little jig, and her joy surprised Eva. Somehow, she hadn't realized how much it would mean to Gram if she went to church.

"Okay, bye," Eva said and hung up the phone. She stood up straight with her arms stretched out wide and spun in a slow circle. "You took it too far. Now I'm going to learn everything I can about your weaknesses, and I'm going to fight back."

By the time eight o'clock rolled around, Eva had calmed down a bit and was wondering if she'd made the right choice. Was she actually going to church? Her stomach flip-flopped as she ate breakfast, imagining herself in the pew next to her grandparents. What would people say? What would she say to people? But the idea of backing out on Gram after she sounded that excited was even more scary. By the time her grandparents' old maroon minivan pulled up on the gravel street in front of Eva's house, she was ready for them.

"Good morning, sweetheart. You look nice," Gram said with a smile when Eva got in the minivan.

"Hi Gram. Hi Gramps."

Gramps was driving, and he glanced back at her as if to prove to himself she was there before putting the van in drive. "You finally drank the Kool-Aid, huh, kiddo?" he said with a smirk.

"Merlin!" Gram said, bopping him on the arm, "Leave her alone and drive." She raised her hand, which was clutching her small purse, and pointed at the road. "We're going to be late anyhow, thanks to your 45-minute routine in the bathroom. Honestly, what do you do in there? You're bald. Things can't take that long!"

"Perfection takes time, honey. You don't think I roll out of bed looking this good, do you?"

Gram scoffed. "Please, honey, we've been married for sixty years. That bathroom is no magic chamber."

Gramps chuckled as he pulled into the gravel parking lot at the church. Eva's heart raced in her chest. *Relax!* She told herself. *You are going to church, not death row.*

But she couldn't relax. Everyone was going to stare at her. She fought the urge to run home. Gram must have sensed her desire to flee, because she laid a hand on Eva's arm. "It'll be fine, Eva. Follow my lead and if you don't know what to do or say, keep silent. Half the regulars don't even sing along or say the prayers. No one will notice."

Eva nodded, and Gram pushed open the big wooden church doors Eva had walked through many times to meet Grace and Alex. Only this time was different. The altar had a spotlight on it. Gram and Gramps dipped their hands in the water and crossed themselves the way Grace had. Eva followed their lead. As the cool water touched her forehead, a vague memory came rushing back to her. She'd done this same thing all those years ago when she came with Gram and Gramps as a little kid. It was weird, a foreign language she'd spoken a long time ago and forgotten.

Her grandparents walked two-thirds of the way down the side aisle and filed into a pew without hesitation. Eva had a sense it was the same pew they sat in all those years ago. Maybe it was the same pew they always sat in. Gramps hung back, letting her pass in front of him so she was sitting between Gramps and Gram. She was glad to have them, one on each side, a fortress protecting her from all the staring eyes.

A lady standing at the front of the church welcomed everyone and announced the first song. As they sang, Eva glanced around. She spotted Alex sitting with his parents, and her heart skipped a beat, surprising her. He looked nice in a button-up shirt and khakis.

She could see Grace's family out of the corner of her eye. They were sitting behind and to the left in the third pew from the back—the same pew they always sat in when they met at church. Maybe that's why Grace always picked it?

Eva glanced around at all the familiar faces from the town she'd lived in her whole life. She couldn't help but wonder how many of them were having the dreams too. Who was chasing their meaning beside her? Who had shut them out forever?

The priest led everybody in an opening prayer. Then a man from the audience read something from the Bible. Gram opened to the page he was reading, and Eva followed along with her eyes as he read. When he was done, she looked up and noticed twice as many people in church as there had been before. How did she miss seeing all of them come in? She glanced around, trying not to gawk, but they were all shockingly beautiful.

Gram scrunched her eyebrows together and tapped Eva's leg. Eva turned to face the front of the church, feeling like a naughty five-year-old. She saw Russell with his head bowed, sitting between two of the young people several rows in front of her. She hadn't expected to see him, but of course he went to church here. He was Catholic, and this was the only Catholic Church in town.

The man reading from the Bible at the front of the church finished the second reading and went back to his pew. Everyone stood while the priest read a story about when Jesus was walking through a crowd and felt power go out of him. A woman had touched his robes, and she was healed because of her faith.

When he was done reading, everyone sat back down and relaxed while the priest talked to them. Some people relaxed a little too much and Eva smiled as she saw their eyes droop into sleep.

But she was drawn to the priests' every word. He talked about how, in prayer, they could imagine themselves as the ones reaching out to touch Jesus's cloak. Eva wondered if she should try it.

When the priest finished talking, two people brought a gold bowl and cup up to the front. While the priests said a bunch of prayers, the beautiful strangers filed up to the front of the church. Some of them smiled and others were looking down as if they were sad. Eva wondered why. Then they all kneeled around the altar.

Everyone in the church, including the people at the front, stood. Then they sat. Then they kneeled a bunch as the priest and the audience said some prayers. The beautiful people were still kneeling at the front, and the people around Eva walked up to the front of the church. As they each stepped up to the priest, he held up a white circle, said something, and handed it to them, and they ate it.

As soon as they put the circle in their mouth, a light emanated from them. Some people's light was super bright and other people's light was dull. Russell was as lit up as a Christmas tree. As each person went back to their seat, a beautiful person went with them. When it was about their turn to go up, Gram whispered to Eva, "Cross your arms over your chest like this, and the priest will give you a blessing rather than the Host."

Eva did what Gram told her. When it was her turn, she stood in front of the priest while he raised his arm over her and said a quick prayer. A warm peace spread over her and sank deep inside. As she walked back to her pew, she spotted Jai'Lune walking beside her. How had she missed her before? Eva smiled and lifted her arm in a little wave. *What are you doing here?* Jai'Lune's face seemed to say. Eva shrugged. Then she chuckled to herself. They always could communicate entire conversations without words. It was coming in handy today.

Jai'Lune followed Eva back to the pew and sat beside her. Every muscle in Eva's body was relaxed, and she smiled. In this moment, with Jai'Lune and her grandparents here, everything was right. Calm even.

Communion must have been the main event because things wrapped up quickly after that. When the last song ended, Jai'Lune grabbed Eva's arm. "You're here!" She was obviously excited, but Eva was glad she didn't pummel her with a bunch of questions.

"Gram, who were all those out of towners? I've never seen any of them before."

"What do you...?" she said, but someone came up to talk to her, and she got distracted.

"Don't worry about that," Jai'Lune said, standing up.

Let's go before we get stuck talking to the old people. She winked. *Did she know something she wasn't saying?* The priest was at the back of the church, shaking everyone's hand as they walked out. "Well, who do we have here?" he asked, shaking Eva's hand.

"Eva," she said in a quiet voice.

"Welcome, Eva. I'm glad you could join us." His smile beamed as if he meant it.

Eva didn't know what to say, so she stared down at a spot on the carpet and said, "Thank you."

As Eva and Jai'Lune walked out of the church, Grace bounced up beside them. "Eva, you came to church!" she proclaimed.

"Yep," Eva said, glancing around, hoping no one noticed what a big deal Grace was making out of it. Gram and Gramps had stopped to talk to someone else, and no one was paying attention to them.

"You look like you're feeling better," Eva commented, and she meant it. Grace's hair was brushed, and the circles under her eyes had almost disappeared.

"I always feel better after church. Don't you? All the icky melts away."

Eva remembered the calm that had spread through her and nodded. "I guess, kinda." Eva glanced around one more time to make sure no one was listening, then she leaned in close to Jai'Lune and Grace and whispered, "I wrote something this morning."

"Okay?" Grace said, as if she wondered what Eva's point was.

"Something for the newspaper."

"Oh. Ooooh," Grace said, dragging out her 'o' with understanding. She glanced at Jai'Lune, concern crossing her face.

"Don't worry, Jai'Lune won't say anything. She's sworn to

secrecy." Grace nodded and pushed her lips together. Eva went on. "It was weird, though, when I was writing it."

"Weird how?" Jai'Lune asked, leaning forward.

"The words kind of... came to me. All I was doing was listening and writing them down. I wasn't coming up with them myself. They weren't... my ideas."

"Strange," Jai'Lune said, eyebrows woven together. Grace crinkled her lips in confusion.

"I know. But when I read it, it was good. You know? It had stuff in there I didn't even know."

"What kind of stuff?" Jai'Lune asked.

"I don't know. I'll email it to you later." Eva turned to Grace. "Maybe we can see if Ellie wants to put it in the paper?"

"That could be good. I think the newspaper deadline is Tuesday. What if we showed Ellie tomorrow? If she thinks it's okay, we could get it in the paper this week."

Eva's stomach was a tiny ninja trying to kick its way out. *This week?* It was soon. But might as well get it over with, right? No reason to wait. "Okay."

Gramps and Gram walked up, and Gram said, "Hi, Jai'Lune." She turned to Grace and asked, "And who do we have here?"

"Grace O'Donnell," Grace said, flashing them that million-dollar smile.

"Are you Spencer and Roberta's girl?"

"Yep!"

"Well, that's a great family. It's nice to meet you."

"Nice to meet you, too." Grace said with a wave and bounced off.

When they got in the van, Gramps turned to Eva. "Well, kiddo, that wasn't so bad, was it? I expect you'll be with us again next week."

Eva hadn't even thought about next week. She wasn't done with this one. "I don't know, maybe."

"We'll pick you up a little before nine, same as today." He turned around, and that was that. Gramps sure had a way about him.

Mom surprised them at Ellie's Cafe for brunch. It was a comforting slice of normal as they ordered their favorite food and chatted. Ever since Eva was little, Gramps loved to tell them stories about the most interesting news he'd heard that week. Today it was all about a wildfire raging across Kansas toward Nebraska. "Towns are being evacuated left and right. They think it might burn through Lincoln this week. I hope they get it stopped before it gets to us."

"Oh, John, you know they will," Gram said.

"How about them earthquakes on the coast? I heard they got waves as tall as buildings afterward."

Eva leaned back and took them in. Gramps had a bald head, tan, leathery skin, and wrinkles deep enough you could stick a nickel in them. Gram's shoulder-length gray hair was twisted in a clip for church. Her shirt was the one Mom gave her for her birthday a few years back. Mom had her dark blonde hair up in a cute, messy ponytail. Her smile caused little wrinkles to form at the corners of her eyes. Eva sighed. The people she loved most were all right here at this table. In that moment, her world was right. Too bad that moment wouldn't last.

Chapter Twenty-Eight

Alex was trying to figure out his English homework when something caught his eye—a flash at the edge of his vision. The lights flickered like they were trying to imitate a strobe light. Alex turned his head, stunned to see his bedroom filled with creatures made of light battling others made of darkness.

He jumped out of his chair and stood in a fighting stance, ready to defend himself. The creatures of light held swords of an even more intense light than their bodies. They wielded them in smooth, practiced motions as they sliced through the shifting shadow creatures as they lunged.

The shadow creatures were the utter absence of light, and the opposite of the figures of light in every way. The light creatures had glistening skin and beautiful humanlike facial features. The shadow creatures were beasts with twisted horns and the pointed nose of an opossum. The swords of light glided in a graceful motion, a delicate dance, while the shadow creatures' movements were jerky and unnatural. Their dark robes shifted, and their mouths were echoing horrible, guttural growls of pure hate. When the figures of light struck the shadows creatures, the darkness exploded into orange embers and disintegrated in a vapor of sulfur that burned Alex's nose.

The smell triggered a memory of Eva standing in her living room with a fireplace poker held high. She'd brought it down on the rabid spirit dog clinging to his back. If she could hit that creepy spirit dog, maybe he could join this battle. Alex glanced around for something to swing and came up with a baseball bat he'd tossed in the corner last summer.

Alex grabbed the bat and was ready to launch when an enormous man appeared in the corner of his room, stopping him in his tracks. The guy had a massive sword of white fire that blazed ten times brighter than any of the creatures of light. His powerful legs and arms were as big as Alex's head, muscles bulging against maroon and gold armor. He glowed like the other creatures but somehow was more solid.

When he entered, the darkness paused and shrunk back. Then the shadow creatures snarled and the hate they were emanating intensified. The gigantic figure swung his sword, taking out two, three, four dark figures with one graceful swing of his sword. One figure after another exploded in a twisted fireworks show.

A wave of hopelessness, despair, and utter hatred washed over Alex, and he turned just as a dark figure lunged at him. "Jesus, help me," Alex said, on instinct more than anything, as he swung. Power vibrated from Alex's hands and reverberated through the bat as it collided with the darkness. The embers were closer than ever as they rained down around him. He covered his nose, but the smell of sulfur still seeped in, burning his throat.

The big guy's sword of fire sliced right past Alex's head. Alex touched his hair to see if it was burning and turned to see the sword plunge into a shadow creature lunging at him. The darkness exploded in embers, and some embers landed on

Alex's skin leaving no marks. The now familiar sick smell of sulfur hung thick in the air.

As the last ounce of darkness was pierced, the figures of light faded from view. All except the big guy. He peered at Alex and nodded, then took a step as if through an invisible doorway and was gone. Alex sat down in his desk chair, blinking. His brain was still trying to comprehend what he saw. The darkness was coming. In fact, it was already there.

Alex's phone buzzed, and he realized the guys online were chatting again. Jakub, a guy in Poland, messaged, 'Tonight we have total lunar eclipse with blood moon. Very rare. Scientists say only last one hour. This third hour and still it goes on. Scientists not understand.'

What Russell said about the scientists not being able to understand the power outages popped into Alex's head. Russell said they couldn't understand because they weren't looking in the right world. *Was this more of the same? Maybe he should say something?* But what would he say? That it could be a sign of a spiritual attack? Alex didn't want Jakub to think he was crazy.

He remembered Jakub telling them he lived in his grandparent's house. It was close to the Auschwitz Concentration Camp. His grandpa had seen the smoke from the Crematorium rising above the camp during World War II. Jakub was having the dreams now. *Did the Nazis open a gateway of darkness with the concentration camp?* Alex shivered. Maybe that's why Jakub was having the dreams.

At basketball camp, after lights out, they told creepy stories. Spencer from England told them on the street in front of his grandparents' house they used to behead people. He was having the dreams now too. And what about Sam? He lived in downtown New York close to where the twin towers fell. He was having the dreams too.

Was everyone who had the dreams living near a gateway of darkness? How many gateways could there be? How far had this spread? *And what happened near Marysburg to open a gateway near them?* Alex had a sense of urgency. This had to be fixed.

He texted Eva and waited for her to respond, but she didn't. Antsy, he tried to think where else he could turn. Russell maybe? He didn't have his number. That's okay. He knew where Russell lived.

~

Russell opened the door as if he'd been expecting Alex. "Come in. Where's Eva?" He peered into the night behind Alex.

"I... it's just me. I don't know where she is. She didn't answer her phone." *Maybe he shouldn't have come.*

Russell nodded and shut the door against the dark with a firm sound. "Okay. Tell me about it."

"About what?"

"About what just happened."

Alex stared at him, stunned. There's no way Russell could know. "What do you mean?"

"I could sense a battle but didn't know specifics. I asked God to send St. Michael the Archangel to defend you in battle. Tell me what happened. Are you okay?"

Alex stared at him, struggling to get his words out. "You... you sensed it?"

"It was vague but strong, as if someone was in danger. I figured it was one of you. When we pray for people, it spiritually connects us, and we can get holy intuitions about each other and pray in real time. It's common, but most people miss the signs or don't know how to cooperate with unspoken prayer requests. I'm like an old ham radio operator, been fine tuned to listen and make sense of the static."

If you say so.

"Tell me. What did you see? What happened to you?"

"I think it was a spiritual attack. It had that horrible smell again."

"The sulfur?"

"Yes." Alex told him everything.

"The big guy you saw is most likely St. Michael. Thank you, Jesus, for sending him. But it concerns me these battles are breaking through the veil more often now and with greater intensity. We need to make sure we do everything we can to protect ourselves. Do you have Scripture hanging on your walls at home?"

Alex didn't pay attention to their decorations, but he tried to do a mental scan of their house. "Maybe? I think so. Mom has little signs and stuff in the bathroom. Prayers on the wall."

"Good, it's important to surround yourself with Scripture. Any verses you love from the Bible. Like blessed objects, it repels the evil. Scripture is a sword, and you can say the Bible verses to defend yourself from the evil. Do you have a crucifix in your room?"

Alex shook his head.

"Get one." It was not a suggestion. It was a command. *Why had Alex come here?* His parents had the dreams, he should talk to them. But the thought of telling his own dad about his experience made him cringe. He realized Russell was saying something.

"If you ever find yourself in this situation again, you can ask for backup the way I asked God to send St. Michael, the big guy with the flaming sword, to defend you."

Alex nodded, numb inside and more tired than ever.

Chapter Twenty-Nine

At school Monday, Jai'Lune and Eva were sitting cross-legged on the hallway floor trying to figure out their English homework when someone's shoes came into Eva's line of sight. She glanced up to see Janet glaring down at her. "Hey, Eva, I heard you went on a date with my boyfriend."

"Alex?" Eva asked. Janet had caught her off guard and she didn't appreciate the way she was standing over her now.

"Yes, Alex. Who else?" Janet rolled her eyes. A small, scaly creature on her shoulder bared its ravenous teeth. Eva recoiled, glancing at Jai'Lune, wondering if she could see the thing. "Well? Is it true?"

"We were just hanging out. He's a nice guy."

"Yes, he's *my* nice guy. And you need to stay away from him."

"Well, technically, you broke up." Why did she say that? The words had snuck out before she thought them through. Her kneecap burst into pain as Janet's foot collided with it. The scaly creature on Janet's shoulder lunged at Eva too, trying to take a hunk of flesh out of her arm. Jai'Lune swung around and knocked it away with her heavy math book. Eva grabbed Janet's foot before she could kick her again.

It threw Janet off balance, and she fell in slow motion, a giant waving its arms. Eva was grabbing her throbbing knee when something solid collided with her face. Janet's backpack, stuffed full of textbooks, reeled back for another blow.

A teacher ran up to stop the fight, and the scaly creature hissed at her, but she didn't notice. "To the office. Both of you. Now."

"Why me?" Eva limped down the hall, followed by a dozen sets of eyes.

Janet and Eva sat in chairs on opposite sides of the principal's lobby awaiting their sentence while the teacher relayed their story. The first bell rang, and people milled around in the hallway. Everyone who walked by gawked at them as if they were fish in a bowl. One guy almost smacked into the wall, craning his neck to stare. *Why was it taking this long? When would someone come get them?*

Finally, Mr. Hurley came out and led her back to his office where he asked, "Eva, do you want to tell me what happened in the hallway this morning?"

Not really. "I was doing math with Jai'Lune when Janet came over. She's mad because Alex and I are hanging out." Eva rolled her eyes, hating how stupid it sounded. How in the world had she gotten sucked into this drama?

"She said something about going on a date with *her* boyfriend. I pointed out that technically they broke up, and she kicked me in the knee. I grabbed her foot so she wouldn't kick me again, which made her fall over on the floor. She swung her bag around and smacked me in the face." Eva touched the puffy spot on her face and pain radiated from it, making her wince.

"You know we don't allow fighting in school."

"I wasn't fighting. I was defending myself!"

"Well, that's not what the teacher saw. She said you grabbed Janet's foot and threw her down. I reviewed our camera footage and I have to say, I'm seeing the same thing. You're a good kid, but we have a zero-tolerance policy for this sort of thing. I'm afraid I must suspend you for two days, Eva."

Eva forgot the pain in her face and sat up straight in her chair. "What?"

"I'm sorry. Again, it's our policy and there's no way around it. I hate to do it, but my hands are tied."

Eva sank down in her chair, wishing she could disappear. "Mrs. Ainsley will escort you to your locker to get your books. We can send your homework with someone. You don't have any siblings, do you?"

"No." *Rub it in, buddy.* "Send it home with Jai'Lune please." She was the closest thing to a sister Eva would ever have.

"Okay, we'll do that. Eva, please don't let anything like this happen again. I'm afraid, if it does, the consequences will be even more dire."

"I'll try." *A little hard to control whether Crazy Janet would attack her again.* Apparently, that was a crime now. So much for innocent until proven guilty.

Janet and her weird, scaly friend both glared at Eva as she walked by. There was so much hate in their stares. She could feel her skin burning with their gaze. She almost expected Janet to trip her, but that would be too obvious. She sensed the next time Janet came for her, it would be much, much more subtle.

Eva was eating a sandwich and staring out the back window when someone knocked on the front door making her jump.

She opened the door, expecting to see Jai'Lune with her homework, but it was Alex.

"Eva, I'm sorry," he said, stepping through the door and grabbing her arms, staring at her face. "I can't believe she did this to you!"

"I'm fine. Geez Alex, she's crazy. How did you ever date her?"

His eyes were dark and brooding. "I'm sorry, I shouldn't have let this happen to you. I'm so stupid. I should've talked to her."

"And said what? 'Hey, if you're thinking of beating up Eva, don't do it?' How could you have known?"

Alex was pacing and Eva realized she was feeling bad for him, which was insane considering she was the one standing there with a nasty black eye. Still, he cared. That was... nice.

She caught him by the arm. "Hey, I'm fine. Don't worry about it. Maybe super-healing is part of this whole spiritual ancestry package. We don't know!" He laughed and his smile made her heart skip a beat.

"Stay for supper?" she asked on a whim. Her mom wouldn't be home for hours, and she was tired of being alone. "You cook, right? You can make me an 'I'm sorry' supper."

Alex stared for a long moment, as if he could see her soul. Then he nodded. "Sure, I'd love that. I can teach you!"

"Wait a minute, that wasn't part of the deal. You cook, I'll ice my face. I'm due for another twenty minutes anyhow."

Eva sat at the table with her feet propped up on a chair and held an ice pack to her face. While she watched Alex cook, she told him about the letter she wrote. They agreed she should show Ellie.

"Oh, I gotta show you this video my buddy sent today!" Alex pulled out his phone. "He lives in Canada, and I guess the northern lights are crazy right now, super bright and going almost all the time. Everyone's saying they've never seen anything like it, but when I watched the video, I saw something else. I'm not gonna say what, I want to see if you notice it, too."

Alex scrolled through a few posts in a group chat then pushed play and held the phone so they could watch it together. Eva saw beautiful lights painting the black sky. The light transformed into angels of all different colors, holding swords in a defensive position in the night sky.

"You see it?" Alex asked, pausing the video.

"Go back a minute and play it in slow motion."

"There," she said, pausing the video. A band of angels in an arch of green and yellow light. Their robes glowed and their swords flashed. Eva clicked play and watched as the hundreds of angels became thousands, creating a band of multicolored lights and shadows.

Chapter Thirty

After Alex left, Eva sat on her couch and wondered what she was going to tell her mom. Things were already weird between them after her mom found out she was talking to Russell. What would this do to their relationship? She leaned back and pressed her flat palms against her face in frustration. Pain shot out from her black eye, making her wince. She let her hands fall beside her and sat there for a minute.

Eva woke up four hours later with a blanket over her. She could hear Mom in the kitchen singing. She couldn't remember the last time she heard her mom sing. She walked to the kitchen and stopped in the doorway, watching her mom drift around the room, preparing a meal. She glanced up and noticed Eva.

"Hey there, Slugger. Let me see that face." She held Eva's face in her hands and gently turned it up to the light. "Ouch!"

"You heard what happened?" Eva sunk into a kitchen chair and braced herself for her mom's reaction.

"I know the basics. Principal Hurley called. You tell me the rest."

Eva told her mom the whole story. "But there's nothing to be jealous of between me and Alex, she's crazy." *Was that true?*

"Okay, well, it sounds like a big misunderstanding and an unfortunate case of getting mixed up in someone else's high school drama. Based on Janet's family history, I believe you. Why don't you go lay down, and I'll make us some Sunday Supper."

On a list of a thousand things her mom could have said, that was the last thing she ever would have expected. Memories from her childhood flooded in. Her mom and her sleeping in on Sunday, relaxing all day and having breakfast for supper. They called it a Sunday Supper. It didn't happen often because of her mom's work, but when it did, it was one of Eva's favorite memories. She winced as the ache of the memory hit her. Things were better left forgotten. Easier to handle that way. She tried to shove down the emotions brewing inside her.

Eva laid down on the couch under an old afghan and her mom called her in when the food was ready. While they ate, she peered at her mom. Sometimes she wished she could freeze a moment, so she could live inside it for a little longer. Their meal was over in a flash. Her mom left for the overnight shift at work, the screen door slamming behind her on the way out.

The next day, Eva waited until she thought Ellie's breakfast crowd would be about done, then headed to the café. When she walked in, Ellie whistled, "Woo-wee. Honey, what happened to you?"

"More like, *who* happened? Janet Moorefield went psycho on me because I've been hanging out with Alex."

Ellie walked around the counter to inspect Eva's eye. "That family's been no-good since her grandpa pulled my pigtails and stomped my foot on the playground. I'm gonna grab you some ice. You get a water and go sit down in that corner booth. I'll be right over."

Eva sat facing the wall, hoping to hide her black eye if

anyone came into the café. A few minutes later, Ellie handed her some ice in a plastic bag wrapped in a towel. Eva held it to her face, even though she wasn't sure it would do any good at this point.

"What brings you here, kiddo?" Ellie asked as she sat down.

Eva pulled the piece of notebook paper from her jeans pocket and laid it on the table in front of Ellie. "This."

Ellie read it in silence, then glanced up. "Well, that's real nice. Did you write it?"

"Sort of."

"What do you mean 'sort of' honey? You did, or you didn't."

Eva told her how the letter came to be. Ellie leaned against the back of the booth. "Well, God must approve of our plan if he's throwing us a bone. If the Lord brings you to it, he'll bring you through it. That's what I always say. Baby, I got a sense he's gonna do just that. I'll bring this to Stan today. It'll be in the paper this week."

"What if people figure out the note was from us? From me?" Eva asked, pulling the cold ice off her face.

"The Lord's will be done. If they find out, we'll take that as our cue from Him to share what we know about the need for prayer."

The thought of talking to people about prayer terrified Eva. "Ellie, I don't know anything about God or prayer. I just went to church for the first time in years. I hadn't even held a Bible until a few weeks ago. I'm not cut out for this."

"Lord, have mercy. Honey, you ain't doing this alone. I got you and your friends do too, but most importantly the Lord got you. It ain't on your shoulders. This here's the Lord's doing." She waved the letter Eva wrote. "The Lord knows. We don't have to lead. We just got to cooperate."

"Maybe?" Eva wished she was as convinced as Ellie.

"Let's see where things go, and you keep praying. You been praying, ain't you?" She stared at Eva with the expression Gram used to give her when she asked if she washed her hands after the bathroom.

"I, uh, maybe? I think so."

"Tell me more," Ellie prodded.

"Well, I'm not sure if I'm doing it right. I don't know if it counts," Eva admitted.

"It don't have to count or not, pumpkin. As long as you speaking to Him, God's listening. After that, it's a conversation between two friends and ain't nobody got a right to judge that. Not even you judging yourself. Let it be and see where it takes you." Eva nodded. Sounded easy enough, but things often weren't as easy as they sounded.

Ellie went on, "For instance, I talk to Jesus in my head sometimes, and sometimes I talk out loud. I tell him what's on my mind—whether I'm excited or mad as a hen. If I'm mad at him, you better believe I'm gonna be talking to him about it. He's big. He can take it."

"I guess."

Ellie put her arms on the table and leaned toward Eva as if she was about to share some big secret. "God doesn't need us to be perfect, honey. If he wanted that, he woulda made robots. He wants a relationship with us. He gave us our own free will. Now he's hoping we use it to choose him, but he ain't never gonna force us."

"It's weird talking to someone I can't even see."

"You kidding me? You kids do it all the time with that texting of yours. Or how about every time you talk on the phone? You can't see the person, but you still talking to them, aren't you?"

"I guess. But the other person talks back."

"Wait a minute." Ellie raised her finger in the air, pushed off the table, and stood up. "I'm gonna grab you something." She bustled off and came back with a fat book in her hands.

"This here's my extra Bible. I want you to have it. It's the Word 'a God. You want to hear him speak? Listen to his Word. Spend a few minutes talking to him. Then open it up and see what God has to say. It's the Living Word. You'll be surprised by what you hear."

Ellie shoved the Bible into Eva's hands, and she grasped it as though it were a plate filled with unfamiliar food. "Thanks, Ellie." Eva stood and handed Ellie the ice pack. "I guess I better get going."

"You're a good kid, Eva. We're gonna be okay." She put her arm around Eva's shoulders and patted her gently. Ellie's kindness collided with Eva's stress, and she burst into tears. She was mortified to be crying in public, but she couldn't stop. "There, there child." Ellie pulled her in for a big bear hug. Her arms were big and safe. She let herself relax into the hug as her tears flowed.

Finally, she got herself together and wiped away the tears with a quick gesture. She grabbed a napkin from the silver container on the table and blew her nose. "Sorry, Ellie. I just..." She trailed off. There were no words.

"It's okay, honey. Nothing better than a good cry. Now go on home and get some rest. It'll be fine, you'll see." Eva hoped Ellie had enough faith for both of them.

She stepped outside, eyes trained on the sidewalk in front of her as fresh tears traced silent paths down her cheeks. A movement caught Eva's attention, and she glanced up to see a giant, grotesque vulture crouched and ready to pounce. It was glaring at her with murderous intent in its black eyes. She held up the Bible and, not knowing the words coming out of her mouth, said, "Jesus, protect me." It was as if a giant bubble formed around her. Its opaque rainbow of colors swirled and moved.

The creature must not have been able to see the bubble, because it pounced at Eva. Its beak hit the bubble first, then its head and wings. Instead of popping, the bubble grew stronger—less opaque and more solid. The creature bounced off the bubble and collapsed backward. It shook its head and worked to get its balance. She watched in frozen horror as the creature tried to come at the bubble from all different angles, but the bubble held strong. Each attempt zapped its energy until it collapsed in a black heap and dissolved into ash.

Eva put her hands down and the bubble dissolved. She forced her heavy feet to carry her to her car. Her tears of a few minutes ago combined with the attack left her completely and utterly exhausted and numb inside.

After her two-day suspension was served, Eva headed back to school. The old, familiar smell of industrial cleaners and sweaty high schoolers rushed to greet her, along with the curious stare of everyone in the school. Jai'Lune went up to Eva and grabbed her elbow, pulling her down the hall. "Oh my gosh, Eva, everybody is talking about you!"

"No, really? I had no idea." Eva's words dripped with sarcasm.

"They're saying how you kicked Janet's butt." A laugh escaped Eva's lips. She didn't do much of the butt kicking.

"No, seriously!" she said in a loud whisper. "Janet's still not back! They said she had some kind of mental breakdown. If you ask me, it's all a sad cry for attention. More head games, you know?"

"I wouldn't put it past her." Eva admitted. Still, she cringed at the thought of having anything to do with causing someone a mental breakdown. She gripped her textbooks like a drowning person clinging to a flotation device. The edges dug into her arms.

As if she could read Eva's mind, Jai'Lune sensed her tension. "It's not your fault, Eva. You were the victim. She's the one who attacked you. I saw the whole thing, and you better believe I've been telling everybody that, too." She believed it. Jai'Lune was loyal to a fault. She never doubted for a second Jai'Lune would have her back. Still, she groaned at the thought of being the center of everyone's attention.

"You know how small towns are, Eva," Jai'Lune said, reading her thoughts again. "You'll be the talk of the town until the next big thing comes along. Then everyone will forget about it and move on to the next drama. You just need to keep your head down and ride this out."

Eva knew Jai'Lune was right. Still, it didn't make it any easier. She mentally willed someone to pull the smoke alarm or something equally mundane to distract the masses. "It'll be fine, Eva. You'll see." She clung to Jai'Lune's words as she plodded through her day. *It'll be fine.* When school was over, she did her usual mad dash for the door, and tried to mentally prepare herself for work.

The next morning, Eva braced for another day of being the talk of the school as she pushed open her front door. The moment she stepped outside, everything had a strange haze to it, as if the airwaves were visible. Electricity hummed through her cross necklace where it rested and an invisible force resisted each step, making it difficult for her to move.

Eva reached back for her front door, but the force of the air was pressing it closed. She put her head down and leaned forward, as if walking into a great wind, as she pressed on toward the school. As she walked, she had the impression of battles flashing on either side of her, a broken movie reel blipping in and out.

Glowing figures were slashing and swinging at grotesque creatures of all kinds. Reptilian monsters, evil dogs like the one that attacked Alex, and faceless spaces of shadow and darkness. It was as if she was walking through a long, invisible tunnel as the battle raged on either side of her. Eva was relieved to see they were all ignoring her, and she pressed on toward the relative safety of the school, never this desperate to get there in all her life.

Finally, she reached the front doors. Eva pulled on them and, to her great relief, the doors popped open. She stepped inside and everything she'd been slogging through was released. She blinked as her eyes adjusted to the light and her mind adjusted to the normal, visible world. To her relief, as she glanced around, she realized people had gone back to ignoring her. It gave her a few extra minutes to get herself together before class.

Two cheerleaders were whispering between lockers close to Eva's. Their conversation drifted out to her. "Do you know who wrote it?"

"I don't know. What do you think they meant by 'time is running out'? Do you think it's a threat or something?" Eva's heart sank. They *were* still talking about her... they just didn't know it yet.

Their whispered conversation went on. "Maybe? What if they put a bomb in our school? Wouldn't that be exciting? We'd probably get a whole week off."

"I heard some kids in New York had a bomb threat at their school, and they were closed for a whole month. They almost had to shut down the school forever."

Eva smacked her forehead with her hand, remembering the last paragraph of the letter she wrote for the paper. *The darkness is coming soon—a blackness this town has never seen.*

When it does, all hell will rain down. If you're not protected, you'll be wiped out. Time is running out to make the right choice. It wasn't meant to be a threat, but now she could see how some people might take it that way.

The cheerleaders left just as Jai'Lune walked up. She twisted her face up in a rotten-milk expression. "What's wrong?" Eva glanced around but didn't answer. Jai'Lune spun the lock on her locker and opened the door, shielding them from other people.

"*You* wrote the letter, didn't you?" she whisper-shouted.

"Yes! Shhh. How did you know? Is it that obvious?" Eva glanced around to see if anyone heard Jai'Lune.

"Only when you wear that guilty, I-did-it face you've got on right now. You know, people think it's a bomb threat, right?"

"I do now, but that's not what I meant by it. You have to believe me."

"I *do* believe you, okay? Just be cool. Maybe people won't find out. Did you cover your tracks?"

"What do you mean, did I cover my tracks? Are we in an old west movie or something?" Eva's sad attempt at humor fell short. Jai'Lune rolled her eyes. "I don't think there's any way people could trace it back to me, if that's what you're asking. I gave it to Ellie, and she took it to the paper."

"Perfect, then you're golden! Lie low and hope for the best." Eva had been doing a lot of that lately. "Seriously, who cares, anyhow? I mean, no offense, but it's just a dumb anonymous letter."

"I guess." Jai'Lune almost had Eva feeling better until she bumped into Grace in the hallway before lunch.

"My dad is on the town council, and they're calling an emergency meeting tomorrow night to talk about the letter," Grace whispered. Her voice was frantic, and her eyes were rimmed with red. "Eva, what are we going to do?"

"Wait, why do they need to talk about it? It's just a dumb anonymous letter," Eva said, borrowing Jai'Lune's words.

"People are nervous, Eva." Grace scratched at her arm in quick jerky movements. "They tried to pressure Stan at the paper into saying who submitted the letter, but he wouldn't tell them. Now they're on some kind of witch hunt to figure it out."

"Oh my *gosh*!" Eva groaned. "How can this be happening?"

Alex walked up and Eva told him about the meeting. "We have to go," he said without hesitation.

"What? Are you crazy?" Grace asked, with wild eyes. "We can't *go* to the *meeting*. They'll know it was us. They'll freak out."

"We have to explain ourselves." Alex shrugged. "They're going to figure it out, eventually. It will be better if we tell them. It's all just a misunderstanding, and we weren't trying to threaten anyone. We were trying to warn them. Remind them to pray and stuff. Maybe this is our chance?"

"I say we ask Ellie first," Grace said, shifting her weight back and forth from one foot to the other.

"Why? Because you think her letter idea was so great?" Alex rolled his eyes.

"Okay," Eva said. "We can't fight, or it'll only get worse. Let's meet at Ellie's Cafe after Alex is done with practice tonight, and we'll get this sorted out."

"Fine." Alex gave Grace the stink eye and stalked off to his next class.

"Fine," Grace said with a roll of her eyes.

Chapter Thirty-One

After practice, Alex took the fastest shower of his life and bolted out of the locker room, still rubbing his wet hair with a towel as he left the school. He wanted to get to Ellie's Cafe and see what she said. Alex had developed a theory. If the angels needed strength to ward off the darkness, maybe if everyone prayed, the dreams and weird stuff would stop happening and his life could go back to normal. Alex was dreading having to tell them, but he was even more desperate to get it over with.

He pushed the door open at Ellie's Cafe and the little brass bell on the handle jingled. Ellie glanced up from her spot behind the pie counter. "Well, look who's here! Are you hungry? Sit down and I'll bring you some pie."

Alex chose the corner booth for privacy. Ellie slid a plate of pecan pie in front of him and an ice-cold water.

"I was gonna bring you a Coke, but I heard Coach don't want you boys drinking pop during the season."

"Thanks, Ellie." He mustered up a weak smile.

Ellie plopped down in the booth across from him. "What is it, honey?" At that moment, Eva and Grace walked in. He waved them over and as soon as Grace sat down, she said, "People think our letter is a threat. They're going to have an emergency city council meeting about it tomorrow night, and we're trying to decide whether we should go."

Ellie sat back and rolled her eyes. "I don't know why folks gotta be so stupid. There's nothing in that letter threatening nobody."

Eva spoke up. "It's the last paragraph that people are worked up about. It says, '*The darkness is coming soon—a blackness this town has never seen. When it does, all hell will rain down. If you're not protected, you'll be wiped out. Time is running out to make the right choice.*' So, of course, they think that means we're going to kill them."

"Well, that's the dumbest thing I ever heard." Ellie snorted.

"I think it's our opportunity to get this thing going. Share what we know and see if we can shut it down. The dreams and stuff, I mean," Alex said.

"Well, I suppose you're right. This might be the opportunity we were waiting for. We gotta go to that meeting."

"I think so too," Eva said. Alex was relieved to know she was on his side.

"A buncha crazy kids is what they are. Maybe I can talk some sense into 'em." Alex hoped so. Maybe Ellie could do all the talking and he'd just sort of be her support. "I'll see you children tomorrow night. Bring your folks with you if you can. Those meetings can get nasty, and you don't need to be dealing with that alone at your age."

They all stared down at their hands at the mention of their parents.

"Well, you told your parents about the dreams, didn't you?" Ellie asked.

They shook their heads and Eva looked up. "Well, Russell

knows, but I didn't tell him. He showed up and asked me if I was having them. He kind of already knew."

Ellie stared at Eva for a long minute. Then she said to all of them, "Tell your parents. They need to know about this."

All three of them nodded, and Alex wondered if the others were thinking the same thing he was. There was no way he was going to run home and tell his parents. That's the last thing he needed was something else to worry about. He couldn't handle it right now.

They stepped out into the crisp evening. Alex breathed in deep, the smell of fall comforting his nerves. The light was fading as day turned to night. He stopped and touched Eva's arm. "Can I talk to you?"

Eva nodded. Grace said, "I gotta go. See you later." Alex wondered if she was still mad at him, but he didn't care, as long as he and Eva were okay.

When Grace left, he asked, "Should we go talk to your dad? Tell him what's going on?" She made a face, and he rushed on. "I thought maybe he should know. Since he was kind of helping us before, too."

"When? The meeting's tomorrow night."

"Let's go now." He hadn't known he'd say that until the words came out of his mouth. But why not get this show on the road?

Eva glanced around. Maybe she was searching for an excuse? After way too many seconds had passed, she said, "Sure, but you're driving. I don't want my mom to see my car there again. It's a whole thing."

"Okay, sure, no problem." They walked to his pickup and Alex got nervous. "You gonna tell your mom about the meeting?"

Eva shrugged. "You?"

"I don't know, probably not. Maybe should though. I read in my dad's journals from high school that both he and mom had the dreams. I'm not sure if that's a good sign or not, considering they've never said anything to me about them."

"They *both* had the dreams? How deep does this thing go in this town?" Eva stared out the window as they passed buildings in the dark.

~

At Russell's, they knocked, and Alex hoped he was home. When Russell answered, his eyes opened wide in surprise. He quickly let them inside. "Well, I didn't expect to see you two. What a pleasant surprise," he said, and he invited them to have a seat on the couch. They told him about the letter and the town hall meeting.

"Well, this all sounds like progress to me. You kids already got further than Eva's mom and I did. I guess all we can do now is pray."

"Yeah, but will you come to the town hall meeting with us, too?" Alex asked. He knew it wasn't his place, but he also knew they needed as many adults on their side as they could get in case things went badly. Or what if they went well? They would need someone to explain to the group that the angels were battling, but they couldn't hold off the darkness much longer. "If people will listen, we need your help to teach them how to fight."

"Maybe we should begin by teaching you two what you can do to join the battle."

Alex turned to Eva to gauge her reaction. Her lips were pressed together in determination, but her eyes were wide with fear as they exchanged glances.

"For starters, you need to understand that we are in a precarious situation. The veil between the visible and invisible world is thinner than ever. As a result, you may be aware of things you couldn't normally see."

Eva scrunched up her nose. "What do you mean?"

Russell paused for a moment, scrunching his face in thought. Then he held up a finger as if he had an idea. "It's kind of like in the morning when the light shines through the window, and you can see all the dust floating in the air. The dust is always there, but most of the time you can't see it."

"Okay," Alex said, thinking of the little specks floating around in their living room as they reflected the morning sun.

"The spiritual world is that way. It's all around us, but we can't see it." Alex glanced around the room. It was weird to think of an entire world around them he couldn't see.

"Remember how I told you our sins poke holes in the veil separating the invisible spiritual world and our visible world?" Alex and Eva nodded. "There are so many holes now, the evil is finding more and more ways to break through."

"The attacks," Alex said.

"Yes, and you might see saints, angels, and demons too, especially when they battle."

"Saints?" Eva asked.

"Yep. Saints are regular human Christians who lived on earth at some point. Because of their faith in Jesus, their death was a doorway into heaven and the invisible spiritual world where they are very much still alive. Even though the spiritual world is invisible to us, because the veil is so thin right now, you might see the saints or sense them occasionally. This will likely happen more often as the veil between the physical and spiritual world continues to wear thin."

"What do they look like?" Eva asked, leaning forward.

"A lot of times they'll look like normal humans, but sometimes their bodies will shimmer with the glow of heaven."

Eva nodded. "I think I know what you mean. I've seen them."

"Me too."

"Okay, good," Russell said. "Your spiritual senses will get

stronger the more you use them, so that's good practice." He turned to Alex. "Like in the weight room. The more you work your muscles, the stronger they get. The same is true for spiritual exercises."

At that, Russell stood up, threw open the door, and Alex watched as his fist collided with a prehistoric beast screeching toward them. The beast's red fangs oozed black tar as it crumpled to the floor at Russell's feet, then burst into embers.

The smell of sulfur burned Alex's nose, and he stood up. "Whoa, how did you know that thing was coming at us?"

Russell shut the door and straightened his blue sweater vest as he walked back to his chair. "You know how sometimes you'll be in a crowd and get a sense someone's staring at you? You glance up and they are? Or how you sense someone is in the room before you see or hear them?" Alex nodded. "That's kind of the physical world's equivalent to spiritual instincts. When evil's approaching, you can almost sense a shift in the air. You'll learn the sensation. When angels or saints are present, you can sense their peace too."

"Now, let's move onto the value of a good perimeter." Russell sounded like Alex's dad. "If you have a good perimeter, it's harder for the evil to break through to you. When it does, it will be weaker from the effort of getting through the way that beast was." He gestured to the floor where the beast had been.

"What do you mean perimeter?" Eva asked.

"The evil can't stand being around holy things like Scripture, holy water, a crucifix. These are defensive weapons we can use to protect ourselves and set up a perimeter. When we have them around, we're creating an environment the evil is uncomfortable in. It drives them away, distracts them, and torments them. If you do a good job setting up your perimeter, it can keep a lot of the evil out. But sometimes a few will sneak through, like that little fella who paid us a visit a few moments ago."

"How do we set up the perimeter?" Alex asked, as if he was playing war.

"Go around your house and your property sprinkling holy water or blessed salt, as you say something like 'I bless this house or property in the name of Jesus Christ.'"

Alex remembered Grace saying something like that. He'd been a Catholic all his life and had never heard or seen anything about this. It made him wonder if it was true, but the attacks made it hard for him to believe it wasn't true at this point.

"Grace told us about holy water, but what's blessed salt?" Eva asked.

"I've never heard of it either," Alex admitted. Was this a normal Catholic thing? *How had he missed it?*

"It's ordinary salt that's been blessed by a priest or bishop. They use it a lot in exorcisms, but we can use it to bless our homes and property too. And you can use the name of Jesus to test the spirits."

"Test the spirits?" Eva asked.

"The Bible says, *'Beloved, do not trust every spirit but test the spirits to see whether they belong to God, because many false prophets have gone out into the world. This is how you can know the Spirit of God: every spirit that acknowledges Jesus Christ comes in the flesh belongs to God, and every spirit that does not acknowledge Jesus does not belong to God. This is the spirit of the antichrist that, as you heard, is to come, but in fact, is already in the world.'*"

"The evil spirits are tricky. They'll try to get you to believe you are seeing an angel or saint when, in all actuality, it's an evil spirit. If they gain your trust, they can get you to do things you wouldn't otherwise do."

"So, we test them," Alex said. "Give them a lie detector test."

"Exactly. Say something like, 'Jesus Christ is the word made flesh' out loud three times. If it's a spirit from God, they will stay. If not, the evil will flee. It can't stand such a proclamation of holiness and truth. This is a good thing to do whenever you sense a spirit, or even when you are nervous or anxious out of the blue for no particular reason. A lot of times, people don't realize it, but that can be the beginning of a spiritual attack."

"Sorry, but that's almost too easy. And why do you have to say it out loud?" Eva asked. Alex was wondering the same thing.

"Good questions! A lot of people don't realize it, but the name of Jesus is powerful. That's why saying Jesus's name in vain, as a swear word, is such a major sin. The name of Jesus literally carries with it all the power and holiness of Jesus."

"And we say it out loud because the evil spirits can't hear our thoughts. They can perceive our emotions and mood and guess or predict what we will do with shocking accuracy, but only God and his angels can hear your thoughts. So, we say it out loud to chase them away."

"I thought you said evil spirits used to be angels. Why can't they hear our thoughts too?" Eva challenged.

"They can only do what God permits them to do. God doesn't allow evil spirits to hear human thought. It's one way he protects us and our free will. The evil only has the power over us that we allow. When we learn to stop cooperating with the evil, life can get a lot better." Russell sounded as if he was speaking from experience.

"And of course, we already talked about praying that the angels have strength. God gives them a boost when we do this. It's part of the free will thing again. When we choose to ask God to power-up the angels, He answers our prayers."

"Set up a perimeter, test the spirits, pray God will give the angels extra strength. Those are the basics. It's what we need to teach the town to do. If they'll listen."

Chapter Thirty-Two

Eva pushed open the screen door, and Mom was standing in the kitchen. *Should she tell her about the dreams and the meeting? Would she listen?* Eva was about to show up at a town hall meeting with Russell and half the town. Everyone would know after that. She didn't have a choice but to tell her mom.

"Mom, can I talk to you about something?"

"Sure, but that tone makes me nervous."

"Let's sit down."

"You're pregnant."

"What? Mom, no!"

"Okay, well, I was just checking." As if that was the worst plausible scenario she could imagine because it happened to her. Eva happened to her.

"Mom, the truth is, I'm having dreams."

"Okay." Trepidation oozed from the word.

"It's not only me. Kids at school are having them too. We told Ellie and..."

"Wait a minute, you told Ellie?" Eva's mom interrupted her.

"Well, uh-huh." Her mom didn't seem to care about the dreams, as if she already knew. She was more worried that Eva told Ellie.

"You should have ignored them. Push them out of your thoughts the second you wake up. They go away. It's not that big of a deal." She was almost pleading now. "Don't get sucked into this, Eva. Not the way I did. It's too much. You're young. You still have a chance."

"It's too late."

"What did you do?"

"We put a letter in the town paper."

"That was *you?*" The anger and fear that filled her mom's face made Eva lean away from her. Her mom stood up and began pacing. "We can fix this. We can fix this."

"How Mom? They're already having a town hall meeting about it tomorrow night."

"What?"

"Townhall. The town's convinced the letter's a threat or something. But I didn't mean it that way. You have to believe me. I'm telling the truth."

"Go to your room. I don't want to see you right now."

Eva got up and walked to her room, deflated. Flip was close on her heels. This is why she didn't tell her mom earlier. She knew her mom wouldn't support her. But if this is how she expected her mom to react, why did it still upset her so much?

Eva was lying on her bed, staring at the ceiling, when her door opened. "I'm going to that meeting with you. I'm late for work." Her mom shut the door firmly behind her.

What was that? She didn't know whether to be relieved or more worried than ever.

~

Eva's phone buzzed, startling her. It was Grace. "Can we talk?"

Eva was curious about what was going on, but she didn't have the energy to go to the church.

"Sure. Want to come here? No one's home but me."

"See you in a minute."

Eva hopped out of bed and headed to the living room to pick up before Grace got there. As soon as Grace walked in, she began talking. "We cannot go to that meeting. We're going to stir everyone up and make them think we're weird."

Oh, like that'd be anything new. But Eva guessed it would be new for Grace. She was used to being popular. Eva didn't have much to lose in that department. Plus, did they have a choice? "This is a small town. If they keep digging, they're going to figure out who wrote that letter, eventually. The longer we wait, the worse it's going to get. I mean, who knows, they could launch a police investigation or something. We don't want that. Are you worried because your dad's on the council?"

It was as if a switch flipped, and Grace burst into tears. The tears built to sobs. Eva wanted to comfort her but didn't know what to do. She patted Grace's shoulder awkwardly. "I haven't told my parents anything. I can't. They'll hate me for this."

"They're your family. They won't *hate* you. It's not like you did anything wrong."

"You have no idea," Grace said. "Dad has these super high expectations for all of us. If we don't do what we're supposed to, he kinda loses it. Tells us how disappointed he is. Goes around the house screaming and throwing things. He's going to freak out if he knows I'm a part of this." This shocked Eva. They always seemed to be the perfect family. *Maybe things weren't always what they seemed.*

"Don't come," Eva said in a rush, desperate to stop Grace's tears.

"What?" Grace asked, staring wide eyed at Eva.

"It's okay, just don't come. Be our silent partner or whatever. It might be nice to have someone on the inside, you know? To hear what people are saying at school and what your dad says when he gets home from the meeting. You could be our undercover spy. What do you say?"

Her tears slowed. "I guess that could work."

The idea had come out of nowhere, but Eva was warming up to it. It would be super helpful to know what was going on in town, especially if they were ostracized after tomorrow. "I don't know why I didn't think of it before," Eva said. "It's perfect."

"You truly think so?" Grace wiped her last tears away.

"Definitely. This could be exactly what we need."

Grace smiled and gave Eva a tight hug. "Thank you, Eva. You saved me."

All day at school, nervous jolts of electricity raced through Eva's veins. She was worried about the meeting. How it would go. What they would say. What her mom would think. After school, she was in her room trying to distract herself when she heard her mom come home. It was early. She never got home at this time of day. Eva went out into the living room. "Is everything okay?" She asked, nervous, thinking of Gramps and Gram.

"It's fine, Eva. What are you wearing tonight?"

Eva glanced down at what she had on—jeans and a t-shirt. "This, I guess."

"If things go crazy tonight, I don't want you looking like something the cat dragged in. You're going to dress up nice. And by dress up, I mean an actual dress."

"A dress?" Eva said, a whiny echo of her five-year-old self.

"It's not going to kill you, Eva. I'll do your hair. It'll be fine."

"Fine." She knew she was on thin ice with her mom right now. Better not push it. She went back to her room and slid the hangers across the metal bar in her closet, searching for something she didn't hate. She remembered a dress Jai'Lune bought her last year. She said it was the perfect color to go with Eva's green eyes, whatever that meant.

Eva pulled the emerald green dress from her closet and slipped it on. Her reflection caught her by surprise. In her mind, she still was an awkward thirteen-year-old, but in the mirror, she looked more like that high school picture of her mom. The emerald dress clung to her hips and her dark brown hair fell past her shoulders, a stark contrast to her pale skin. She shook her head and turned to finish getting ready.

Eva sat on the bench in the bathroom, the way she used to when she was little, while her mom did her hair. The tugging and brushing and twisting made her wince and the old phrase her mom used to say came back to her. *No pain, no gain.*

Her mom worked in silence. After an eternity, she stepped back to admire her work. "Not bad." She picked up a mirror and handed it to Eva.

Eva positioned herself to see her full reflection in the big mirror. "Wow, Mom, that actually looks really nice." The surprise in her voice bounced off the small bathroom walls.

"Well, does that shock you I might actually be good at something?" Eva's mom scowled, but underneath she wondered if there was a little satisfaction lurking. "Truth be told, I forgot how good I am at this." She chuckled, surprising Eva. "Maybe I should do my own hair once in a while."

"We have plenty of time now," Eva offered.

Eva's mom glanced at the clock. "I guess we do." Setting her jaw in determination, she sat down to do her hair. Thirty minutes later, they were walking out the door. Eva's nerves had calmed while she was getting ready. When she saw the cars lining both sides of Main Street for blocks, all her nerves came rushing back stronger than ever.

"Why are this many people here?" Eva asked her mom, the pit in her stomach growing. The meeting was going to be packed. "I thought it was going to be only the council."

"It usually is, but anybody can go. Most people don't, because the meetings are boring, but apparently, your little letter has caused quite a stir." Mom was stunning with her hair and makeup all done, but her lips were pressed together, and her forehead was wrinkled with worry.

Eva pressed her back hard against the seat of the car and sank down, almost out of sight. She wished she could disappear.

"It'll be fine," her mom said, pushing her lips together.

Mom pulled into a parking spot a couple blocks from the town hall entrance and they got out. Other people were walking up to the building and one of them was Russell. Eva's entire body tensed. Her parents hadn't seen each other since that night on his porch. But to her astonishment, Russell walked right up to them. He smiled at her and then his gaze shifted to her mom.

Her mom's face flushed, a small smile tugging at the corners of her mouth. *What in the world?* Eva was expecting her to verbally assault Russell and here she was acting like a shy school girl. What was happening in this world?

"Russ," she said on an exhale. "You're here."

"Of course. No way I'm letting you go in there alone."

All three of them walked into the town hall together. Eva realized it was the first time she'd gone anywhere with both her parents her entire life and her breath caught in her chest. Ellie and Alex were saving seats for them near the front. Alex's parents were nowhere to be seen. *So, he didn't tell them.*

As they walked down the center aisle, every set of eyes

turned to Eva and her parents. She wondered if they'd be turning their way for another reason soon.

"Well now there's a sight for sore eyes," Ellie said, when they sat down. She pointed at Eva's mom and Russell. "Seeing you two together, I feel twenty years younger." She smiled, and Eva stared at her parents. They were sitting close enough their arms were touching, and if you didn't know better, you might think they were a couple. Russell had shaved and put on a button-up dress shirt. He was as handsome as her mom was beautiful. Hope tried to bubble up inside her at the chance they could be a family, but she pushed it down with a practiced hand. She'd learned a long time ago that hope was a good way to get hurt.

Chapter Thirty-Three

Alex couldn't take his eyes off Eva. The green dress she was wearing made her eyes glowing emeralds. Her hair cascaded in loops and curls, and she smelled good. When she glanced up and caught him staring, his face burned with embarrassment. He nodded, then looked away. Ellie was sitting between them, and she smirked and patted Alex's leg. He was glad Ellie was there with them. Alex didn't have the nerve to tell his own parents, and he hoped they wouldn't hear he was at the meeting until he figured out how to tell them.

The town council sat at the front of the room. There were four men and one woman. Alex recognized them all from around town. The guy in the middle banged his gavel on the table as if he thought he was a Supreme Court judge. But he was just Roger, the guy who owned the local meat locker. "Can I have your attention, please? Quiet down. We're about to get started."

It took a few moments and a couple more bangs of the gavel, but the roar of chatter in the room died down to a dull murmur. "We are here tonight to discuss the threatening letter addressed to our town in the local newspaper."

"Let's get 'em boys," some hothead in the back said. "Ain't nobody threatening my town. We got to defend ourselves."

Alex mentally rolled his eyes but kept his face still, trying not to bounce his knee. He fidgeted with an old paperclip he'd found in his pocket.

"That's enough," Roger said with a smirk. "Stan, will you please stand up and explain to us again why you can't disclose who wrote the threatening letter?"

Stan, the owner of the newspaper, stood up nervously fidgeting with the hat in his hands. "Well, it's simple. I can't say who gave me that letter because I told them I wouldn't. A man's only good as his word." The crowd murmured. A few men in flannel shirts with their arms crossed in front of them leaned back in their chairs and nodded. Other people glared at Stan.

"You promised someone you'd help threaten our town?" Roger boomed. "And now you can't tell us who that someone is?"

"Come on, Stan. You're better than that. You owe this town the truth," came another voice from the crowd.

"Well, I... uh." Stan shook his head and stared down at his hands.

"You think loyalty to this terrorist is more important than the safety of the people sitting in this room? The children living in this town?"

"It wasn't a terrorist," Stan said in a quiet voice. Alex's stomach turned at seeing Stan take the fall for them. He couldn't stand it. It wasn't right. Alex popped to his feet, stared Roger in the eye and said with a confidence he didn't have, "It was me."

The entire room turned their attention to Alex. As their stares dug into Alex, his face grew warm. He was probably blushing a deep red. He hated it, but he held his ground. He might not be a man yet, but he could act like one.

"Take a seat, son. We know you wouldn't do this. You don't have to take the fall."

"Why not?" Alex said, baffled at Roger's refusal to believe him.

"You've got too much to lose. The chance at a football scholarship. Your future. You're smarter than to risk it all. You don't want to get mixed up in this."

"Come on," someone in the crowd said. "Whoever wrote this letter, you gonna let this kid take the fall for you? Stop being a coward and turn yourself in."

Off to the side, someone said, "Coward? You're a fine one to talk. Ever since your family came to town you been raising packs 'a cowards."

"Come on over here and I'll show you how coward I can be."

"That's enough," Roger warned.

"Actually, it was me, sir," Eva said. Alex winced and turned to see her stand up tall, staring Roger in the eye. Her mom tried to tug her down, but she stood firm. "I wrote the letter."

"Explain yourself, young lady." Roger said with narrow eyes. Apparently, he had no problem believing Eva could be guilty.

"I didn't mean for it to be threatening. In fact, it was just the opposite. I meant for it to help. To tell people what's coming and how to stay safe."

"And what exactly *is* coming?" The lady on the council spat at her.

Eva took a deep breath and responded, "Evil."

The room erupted, everyone talking at once. Roger banged his gavel and bellowed, "Quiet!"

It quieted down a bit, and he asked, "What do you mean 'evil'?"

Russell stood up. "When we were in high school, I told you the same thing, but you didn't listen then, did you?

Maybe you're older and wiser and ready to listen now? Cause our time is almost out."

At that, the entire room erupted. Alex heard someone shout, "Not this again!"

"This town's had enough of that talk. We don't need it now."

Others said, "Let them talk. Maybe if we listened, we could get this over with once and for all."

Roger turned on Russell, a bear preparing to attack. "It wasn't enough you knocked up Rachel and ran off, Russell? Now what? You're back to mess things up for our entire town?" As he spoke, Roger's voice grew to a roar, drunk on his own power, and the crowd quieted down to watch the show.

"I'm doing what I should have done a long time ago," Russell said. "Standing behind Rachel and Eva, doing everything I can to help this town before it's too late."

Roger opened his mouth to speak, but Ellie stood up. "Uh-huh, Roger, now that's enough."

Roger was a naughty school boy reprimanded by the teacher. "What do you mean, Miss Ellie?"

"Don't be pretending you're not a Dream Haver. You might not know what those dreams meant, but I do." Roger was stunned into silence. His face went red, and he shut his mouth with a snap. Ellie went on, "Far as I can tell, the dreams are God's way 'a telling us to grab hold tight to Him, because things about to get rough. This isn't just a story, it's a major attack gonna be launched. We can expect some frightening darkness headed our way. We gotta do what we can to stop it." *Ellie knew more than she was letting on before.* "God will protect us, but we gotta know how to grab hold tight 'a him. Most of you folks in this town ain't never been trained proper."

Ellie commanded the room in a way none of the rest had. Now she turned to face the crowd. "It's not brain surgery here, people. We can teach you how to help save this town. Defend yourself and grab hold 'a the hand of the real and living God. If there's anybody wants to learn, come to the café tomorrow night at six o'clock. Bring your kids. Bring your parents. Your friends. Whoever wants to come is invited, no matter what church you go to. Food's on me, and you're all welcome. I'll be giving out free kits to help you through too. Now, raise your hand if you plan on coming. I want to get a count." After a moment of hesitation, a few people raised their hands.

Alex smelled sulfur and sensed a shift in the room. Someone said something in the crowd and a fist fight broke out, but Alex was too distracted to notice the details. Above the crowd, an invisible curtain drew back revealing a battle between creatures the color of night and day. Light and dark flashed and swords clanged.

Beside him, Alex heard Russell and Ellie praying as they held up crucifixes the way knights in battle hold up swords and shields. Embers burst above the crowd and rained down, but they were unaware of the invisible battle raging above them.

Alex turned to Eva. She could see it, too. Her head was tilted back, and her arms were up to defend herself. There was an expression of wide-eyed horror on her face. The crucifix resting on her collar bone glowed orange.

Russell moved Eva's mom behind him in a motion of protection, as dark wisps formed thick pillars of smoke throughout the room. "We need to get out of here. The darkness is about to break through," Ellie said above the roar of what had become a full-out brawl in the town hall.

Russell nodded and said to their group, "Don't engage with anyone... or anything. Walk straight out and pray for protection." What was he worried about? Would the evil creatures hurt them in front of all these people? Alex didn't think they would, but he didn't want to find out.

Their group moved together, Russell leading the way, holding up his crucifix in front of them as they walked. When they were almost to the door, an old farmer separated from the crowd and came at them, a dark shadow figure close behind as though for reinforcement. Russell said something Alex couldn't hear, and the farmer took several steps backward, glaring at them as he did.

When they made it to the sidewalk, Eva took a ragged breath. "Is this it, Ellie? Is the darkness coming for real right now?"

"I don't know, child, but we need to get to the café. Then we'll talk. I got all the supplies we gonna need to weather this storm if it's here."

They split up and headed to their vehicles. Alex jogged up to his pickup, thinking how much his world had changed in the few minutes since he'd parked it there. He drove faster than he should to Ellie's Cafe, his heartbeat pounding in his ears. *Was this it? Was it happening right now?*

Chapter Thirty-Four

Eva and her mom got to the café as Ellie was unlocking the front door. Everyone else was pulling up, too. Ellie held the door open for all of them as they rushed inside. She locked the door behind them and paused for a moment, staring out into the night.

When Ellie turned around, her face was set with determination. "Eva and Alex, will you come help me with something in the basement, please? Russell and Rachel, can you pull all them blinds closed fast and push the tables together in a long line?" Eva's mom and Russell exchanged glances and got to work. Eva and Alex followed Ellie to the back of the diner and down the steps to the dark, musty basement.

When Ellie flipped on the lights, Eva saw a large room with new vinyl flooring. Pillows and blankets were strewn around in piles, and there was a wooden cupboard with a crucifix and a statue of Mary in the center of the room. Bed sheets had been duct taped over all the windows. *What was this place?*

"Ellie?" Eva said, hesitantly.

"Over here." She motioned for Alex and Eva to follow her.

"Grab these boxes. They'll be heavy. We gotta make the kits. I thought we had more time. I pray to Jesus we ain't outta time yet."

Eva and Alex took several trips, carrying the heavy boxes out of the basement. When everything was upstairs, Ellie organized them into an assembly line of sorts.

"People gonna need certain things to survive the days of darkness without losing their sanity. Or their soul. We gotta put together these kits now and pray God's angels can hold off the evil until after tomorrow night so we can hand them out."

Ellie ripped open a box labeled beeswax candles with the word 'blessed' handwritten in permanent marker on the box. Other boxes were filled with little bottles of holy water, like Grace had given Eva and Alex.

As they assembled the kits, Eva noticed she wasn't the only one who kept stealing glances outside to see if the darkness was upon them yet. At the town hall, when the chasm opened over the crowd and the pillars of darkness formed, she thought that was it for sure. But now she wasn't as sure. Was the darkness going to seep in gradually over the next few days? Was the town hall meeting a tremor before the big event? "What do you think will happen if the darkness comes, Ellie?" She needed to know what she was bracing for.

"I don't know, honey. Lots of predictions. Some crazier than others. Some more specific. But saints been talking about a period 'a darkness heading our way for centuries. Sure, feels like it's almost here." Eva shivered.

"I can't believe you offered to host everyone here tomorrow," Alex said.

"I know. It just kinda... came out. Felt like the Holy Spirit was leading me, so I went with it," Ellie admitted. "Gonna be a lotta fried chicken if people show up. You children coming, right?" She eyed Eva and Alex with one eyebrow up in an expression that said it was not a question.

"Of course," Eva said.

"I'll be here," Alex responded.

"I expect I'll see you here too, Rachel and Russell. Am I right?" Eva smiled at Ellie, bossing her parents around.

Eva's mom cringed and said, "I'll have to check my work schedule." Ellie put her hand on her hip and stared at Eva's mom through bushy eyebrows. She quickly added, "But I'm sure I can figure something out."

"That's more like it, honey. The Lord will take the place you give Him, but last place ain't no place for the Lord."

"Amen to that!" Russell said, stepping in to take the heat off Eva's mom. "I'll be there with bells on. Ellie, how many people do you think this café can hold?"

"I don't know. Maybe a hundred in that big room upstairs and fifty here in the dining room if we pack them in like sardines and pray the fire marshal don't come."

Russell was energized, talking faster than normal, and using his hands to emphasize his words. "Okay that's our goal, one hundred fifty people. What's the best way to get the word out to people who weren't at the meeting?"

"Gossip gonna do a lot for you right there," Ellie pointed out. "Course it's always the things you want to spread that don't, so maybe not."

"Online," Eva said. That's where people are. "I could post an event. Send messages. That sort of thing. I bet Jai'Lune would help. She's good at that stuff."

"I'll hang up signs around town to get the older crowd interested," Ellie said.

"Great," Russell said. "How about you, Alex? Any ideas?"

"Um, I could message my football team. I don't know if they'll listen, but that's about thirty people right there."

"Okay, great," Russell said. "We have a plan. Let's pack this café full."

"Think we'll make it until then?" Eva asked, sneaking her

thousandth glance outside. It was dark, but the streetlights illuminated the area. She was pretty sure it was an ordinary night, not the darkness that threatened to break through in the town hall.

"Oh, I expect we will," Ellie said with a glance of her own outside. Eva wondered if Ellie was as confident as she sounded.

They finished packing the kits and Ellie made sure they each had one to take home. "If anything goes south, get your little selves to me and I'll take care 'a the rest. Everything we gonna need is right here in my basement. Food, blankets, other supplies."

They all exchanged glances and Eva gave a nervous laugh. Then it was time to leave. "Eva, do you want a ride home?" Alex asked. Eva's mom nodded it was okay, so she said yes.

When she'd climbed up in his pickup, Alex turned to her. "You look beautiful tonight."

She blinked her eyes a few times, thrown off. She'd expected him to say something about the town hall meeting or the darkness, not this. After a few beats, she managed to say thank you.

He nodded, started the truck, and eased out of the parking lot. "I was freaking out during the meeting." He admitted.

"Me too, but then you stood up." She stared at him. "Why'd you do that? Why not keep your mouth shut and let Stan handle it?"

"I couldn't stand to see him take the fall for us. You stood up too," he pointed out.

"I couldn't let you take all the fall."

"Ha, thanks." He smiled, and she enjoyed the way it made her feel.

"Your parents weren't there," she pointed out. "You haven't told them?"

"Not yet. I can't bring myself to do it, you know? I figured I'd see how tonight went and then decide if I was going to tell them or not. No sense getting them all riled up if it wouldn't come to anything."

"They'll find out after tonight."

"I know," he said with a cringe. "I'm not looking forward to it. Grace didn't come."

Was he trying to change the subject? "She told me last night she's scared." Eva told Alex about her idea to have Grace be their spy.

"Good thinking," he said, his dark eyes brooding. She wondered what else he was thinking.

Chapter Thirty-Five

As Alex drove home, he began to sweat. Even though his parents weren't at the meeting, someone would have called them by now. They'd know he was there. He debated whether to go straight to Pops' house. No, he needed to face this head on. Like a tackle, it'd be worse if he ran from it than if he put his shoulder down and met the problem with all his strength.

It didn't surprise Alex that his dad was waiting up for him in the living room. He stood as Alex walked in. "Heard there was a big town hall meeting tonight. You acting foolish sure didn't help."

Alex's muscles stiffened, and he braced himself for the impact of his dad's words. He set the kit Ellie gave him down on the floor. "Ellie sent this for you in case there's trouble." *Time's up, Alex. Tell them what you did.* "Dad, I can explain."

"Oh, I'm sure you can. You got nothing but explaining to do, boy. But you ain't got no clue what you're stepping into."

"Dad, I'm having the dreams." Alex's gaze begged his dad to understand. He'd had the dreams too, surely he knew how hard it was.

Alex hadn't noticed his mom in the room until she spoke in a whisper. "What do you mean, Alex?"

"Mom, I know you had the dreams too. Please, we have to do something. We can't let this, this thing come at us. We need to defend ourselves."

"Shut your mouth, boy, before I have to shut it for you." His dad stalked toward him.

"Don't..." Alex's mom said, and his mind registered the fear in her voice. His dad could be unpredictable when he got mad, but Alex wasn't afraid. His blood was boiling.

"Why didn't you tell me?" He glanced at both his parents.

"We hoped they wouldn't happen to you." His mom said. She was crying now. "We just wanted it to stop."

"Be quiet. We don't talk about that nonsense in this house."

"You had them too, Dad," Alex pressed, challenging his dad. "Why didn't you tell me? Try to help me? Or at least warn me. You're always talking about tactical advantage. Why'd you keep enemy information from me?"

"You don't know what you're talking about, son. You think you have all the answers? Russell Smith got messed up in all this and see where it got him. Left your little girlfriend without a father. Her mom to scrape by. Pathetic."

"Don't talk about him that way." Before his brain had a second to realize what he was doing, Alex shoved his dad.

"You wanna go, boy? I can still take you down. Maybe that's what you need, someone to put you in your place."

Rage took over Alex's vision. Maybe it was all the helplessness he'd been feeling lately, or the exhaustion and frustration, but something inside him snapped and it was all directed at his dad. It took all his energy to hold back a punch. He needed to get out of there before he did something he couldn't take back. With a last glance at his parents, he turned to bolt out of the house.

His dad's angry voice chased him out of the house. "You're not gonna live under my roof and get mixed up in all this nonsense. You best let it go or don't bother coming back."

His mom's tear-soaked, "No," stabbed his heart as he bolted out the door. He hopped in his pickup and tore down the driveway, desperate to escape. Alex didn't know where he was going until he pulled up in front of Eva's house. He pounded on her front door, and she threw it open. "Alex?"

"My parents know. I can't go back there."

"What?" She tugged him inside.

"My dad and me. We fought, and he said to quit all this, or I can't come back." Alex's heart was pounding in his ears.

Eva wrapped her arms around him. "It'll be okay, Alex. We'll figure this out. We'll figure it out."

He put his arms around her and leaned into the hug. She was his safe place. "I don't know what to do anymore," he said into her hair. He released her and paced the living room. "I mean, I'm having these dreams for a reason. What am I supposed to do? Ignore them? Why didn't they tell me they had them too? Why can't our family *talk* about anything like normal people?"

"They'll come around," Eva said. He wondered if she believed it. "Maybe you can stay at Russell's until then."

At that moment, it struck him, he was homeless. He had no place to go. The thought made him sick to his stomach. Alex knew he could ask Pops, but he didn't want to put him in the middle of this mess.

"Sit down. I'll get us something to eat," Eva said, and he sat, hands on his knees, trying to force his heart to slow down. A few seconds later, she came back with cookies and milk. They sat on her couch facing each other while they talked. "We can't assume everyone who had the dreams feels the same way we do. Some people might be ashamed or scared and reject them. This has been dividing our entire town for generations. It's not going to change on a dime, but it can get better if we don't give up."

He knew she was right. He just didn't expect it to hurt this much. "Sleep on the couch tonight. We'll figure something out in the morning, okay?"

He nodded. "Your mom won't care?"

"She's working the night shift. Be gone before six, and we don't have to find out."

"Thanks, Eva."

She nodded and left the room.

Chapter Thirty-Six

Eva tried to ignore the fact that Alex was sleeping on her couch and let herself drift into sleep. That night, she had the tornado dream again, but it was different this time. When she talked, a few people listened. They stood up, turned around, and followed her to safety.

When Eva woke up the next day, for the first time, the dream left her with a lingering hope, not dread. She didn't let herself push the hope away. Who knew, maybe the hope was a sign they were headed in the right direction. Maybe they could stop this thing yet.

Eva woke Alex up before her mom got home, and he left for the weight room to burn off some steam. Then she called Grace.

"Hello? What time is it?" Grace sounded groggy, and Eva glanced at the clock. Whoops, she'd forgotten how early it was.

"Sorry, it's six. I was nervous to hear what your dad said about the meeting last night."

"He was mad." Eva imagined Grace rubbing the sleep from her face. "Said your dad was back in town causing trouble again, and it was déjà vu. The whole town is losing its mind all over again."

Eva cringed. "Well, that doesn't sound good. The meeting got crazy. We slipped out before it was done. But Ellie invited everybody to her café tonight to learn how to protect themselves from the darkness. You wanna come?"

"Eva I can't, remember? I don't want to get involved or my cover will be blown."

Eva knew it was all part of the plan, but she was worried Grace was pulling away from them. "Grace, this is our chance. The moment we've been waiting for. Doesn't a small part of you feel obligated to help these people? I mean, you're having the dreams too."

"Eva, I told you, I can't tell my dad. It's complicated. Our whole family is... complicated." In a rush, Grace said, "Can I tell you something, Eva?"

"Sure."

"I kinda figured out a way to block the dreams. I stop thinking about them the minute I wake up. I shut down that part of my brain. It's hard to explain, but lately I haven't had the dreams or seen or experienced anything weird."

"Shutting them out isn't necessarily a good thing, Grace. What if they're from God?"

"Don't worry. I'll still go to church on Sunday. I just won't open myself up to the dreams, you know? It makes my life easier, and that's what I need right now. I'm not strong the way you are, Eva."

"Are you kidding me? I'm not strong." Eva was an anxious mess. "Grace, don't give up on this yet, okay?"

"Maybe, Eva. I gotta go. I'll talk to you later, okay?"

Eva was deflated as she hung up the phone and she reached in her mind to grab hold of the hope she'd had before the call. She made herself wait until seven to call Jai'Lune. When she picked up, it surprised Eva how awake Jai'Lune sounded. "You're energetic for seven on a Saturday."

"I've had a ton of energy lately. I woke up early for no reason. What's up?"

"Can you help me put some stuff online about an event at Ellie's tonight?"

"Sure! Be over soon."

Eva hung up, relieved she had Jai'Lune to lean on. Russell's words came back to her, "We're stronger together." That might be true.

Chapter Thirty-Seven

Alex needed something familiar, and there was nothing more familiar this early in the morning than the weight room. He'd been coming here every morning for over five years. He was grateful it was Saturday. It meant he had the place to himself. He needed a place to just be. *What was he going to do now that he couldn't go home?* Maybe Eva was right. He could stay with Russell for a few weeks. Early signing period for choosing a college would be here before long. He was pretty sure his dad wouldn't let that go by without getting him home to influence his decision.

Alex worked through his routine without thinking. The strain of his muscles felt good, and it helped him get into a zone where memories of the meeting last night couldn't get through. When he was done, Alex took a shower in the locker room and put on the fresh pair of clothes he always kept in his locker. He rubbed his hair dry and headed back to Eva's house.

Eva smiled when she answered the door and let him in. Alex had just settled on the couch with her when there was a sound at the door and Jai'Lune walked in. She was wearing some kind of flowy purple shirt and cutoff pants with flip-flops, and she had a smile the size of the Grand Canyon on her face. "Oh, hi, Alex."

"Hey," he said with a little wave, unsure what else to say.

Eva gave Jai'Lune a handful of cookies and offered her a glass of milk. Then they got to work getting the online events set up while he worked on texting the football team. They might think he was a weirdo, but that was nothing new.

A few hours later, Jai'Lune checked in to see if they were getting any traction online. "Wow, it's blowing up! People are asking a bunch of questions and tagging friends from everywhere. We better get to responding!"

"Really?" Eva asked, sounding amazed.

"You've officially gone viral and, like two hundred people said they're coming."

"What? The café's not big enough," Eva said, grabbing her computer.

"You've got some haters too." Jai'Lune winced. "All publicity is good publicity, though, right?"

Eva read the comments out loud. The first few were friendly. "If those children are brave enough to stand up at that meeting and be torn to pieces by a bunch of adults, they must have something important to say. I'm going. Plus... free food. Just saying."

Jai'Lune pointed to the screen. "A ton of people liked that comment and replied with similar messages saying we piqued their interest, or they want to know more. They can't wait, or this is just what they needed."

See that one? Jai'Lune pointed at another comment and Eva read it out loud, "Stay away, people. It's all a lot of lies and head games. You'd be better off reading your Bible at home than joining up with this cult."

"Why is Grace's dad leading the pack of haters? I thought she was on our side," Jai'Lune asked.

"That's all hush, hush now," Eva explained. "She's scared to tell her parents."

"I don't blame her," Alex admitted. He would have loved to avoid that little scene with his parents, but he couldn't leave Eva high and dry.

"You're coming tonight, right, Jai'Lune?" Alex asked.

"Obviously! I wouldn't miss Ellie's fried chicken, and all the other stuff too," she said with a wave of her hand and a smirk.

Chapter Thirty-Eight

Alex and Eva got to Ellie's diner about 4 o'clock to help with setup. As they stepped into the warm café, the delicious smell of Ellie's fried chicken, mashed potatoes, and gravy welcomed them. Ellie was in full preparation mode, bustling around getting everything ready, and she gave them both a job to do. Russell showed up and, to her astonishment an hour later, Eva's mom did too.

"Now sit down and have a bite to eat. I don't know if I'll have enough, and I don't want my main folks going hungry. Plus, you surely won't have time to eat once they all pour in," Ellie said.

"Online, it says over two hundred fifty people are coming," Eva said.

"Oh Lord, help me." Ellie fanned herself. "Eat, eat, eat." She waved her hands for them to sit down. "Well, pray, then eat."

Ellie grabbed Eva's hand, and everyone followed suit around the table. While they were reciting the prayer, Eva opened her eyes and peeked around. She noticed Russel squeeze her mom's hand, and her mom's lips turned up at the sides in a tiny smile.

Eva stared at Russell. His eyes were closed, and his hair fell forward a bit on his face. She smiled, wondering if he was past due for a haircut because he didn't want to deal with the chatty local barber. He was wearing what she now thought of as his signature sweater vest, and she realized it was good to have her father at the table with them. Father. That was something she'd have to get used to. She still couldn't believe he was in her life and maybe, just maybe, to stay.

Eva's life had flipped upside down over the last few weeks, as if it were changing with the seasons. But instead of winter, maybe she was heading into spring. Everything was full of new beginnings and hope. She no longer was bored or lonely. She wasn't scared the way she had been in the early days of the dreams. Instead, she was at peace, comforted by the presence of the people sitting at this table. Her people.

They ate in a cloud of nervous anticipation, wondering how the night would go. When they were done, Ellie gave each of them a job in an assembly line to feed the masses. Eva handled the mashed potatoes. Ellie instructed her on how full to fill the ice cream scoop she was using to serve them. "Not too much, you hear? We don't have room for error." Eva nodded, then smiled as Ellie gave Alex strict instructions on how to dish up the corn.

Gramps and Gram were among the first to arrive at the café. Eva smiled and slipped out of line to hug them tight. They grabbed their food and sat at their usual table. More and more families, couples and single people poured into the café, finding places to eat on the main floor and in the large gathering room upstairs. "Dear Lord, we gonna run outta food," Ellie worried.

Russell smiled. "It's okay Ellie. They're here for spiritual food, not fried chicken."

"Well, child, I suppose you're right, and we sure got plenty 'a that, don't we?"

When the upstairs and main floor were full, Ellie opened the basement and people filled in down there. The food never ran out. There was plenty for everyone and a little left over. When they finished serving, Ellie and Russell split up. Russell headed upstairs to talk to the people up there and Ellie stayed on the main floor. They'd both talk briefly to the crowd downstairs when they were done.

Eva and Alex settled in at the table with Gramps and Gram to listen to Ellie talk. A lot of what she said was similar to what Russell had told them. She explained how to set up a spiritual perimeter, test the spirits, and pray God would strengthen the angels for battle. It was clear Ellie and Russell had compared notes and discussed what they'd say. They both wanted it to be a unified, concise message people could understand.

At the end of her talk, Ellie held up one of the bags they'd put together the night before. "We made a kit for you, one per household. If something goes down, close your doors and windows, and cover them up as best you can with sheets, blankets, curtains, whatever you have. Light the blessed beeswax candle. When you do, nothing can put it out, not even the evil. But be warned, if you can't get that candle lit, it might be what's going on in your own heart. The candles can only be lit by a believer of the mercy of Jesus."

She held up a small plastic bottle. "This is holy water. Sprinkle it around your home, especially by the doors and windows. You can also use it to bless each other. From now on, I want you to make sure you have enough food and water at your house to last you three days. I don't know if we'll have power, so blankets 'a good idea, too."

"There's a crucifix in your kit. Set it on the table beside your candle and gather around it as you pray. Ask God to strengthen the angels for the battle raging outside. To pass the time, read any spiritual books you have, especially the Bible. Pray the Rosary or do whatever you can to keep your thoughts on holy things and repentance. Each kit has a few St. Benedict bracelets, too. Wear them."

"And remember, no matter what happens, do not open your doors or windows. The evil will try to trick you and deceive you to lure you outside. But anyone who goes out because of curiosity will die. And I want you to be surviving, you hear? Do not go outside. Now, anybody got questions?"

Someone by the windows said, "We're not Catholic, we don't pray to angels."

"Don't pray *to* the angels. Pray to God. Use your free will choice to ask *him* to give the angels extra strength so they are stronger for battle."

Someone else shouted, "If God wanted the angels to have extra strength, he woulda given it to them."

Ellie took a deep breath. "Honey, it's free will. We used it to get ourselves into this mess and now God's giving us a chance to use it to help get ourselves out. Pray or don't. It's your choice. And we're about to experience the result of what we choose."

After Ellie and Russell were done talking, people filtered out. Some drew their eyebrows down in annoyance. Others had open-mouthed confusion or intrigue. But each family took the kit that was offered to them. A few thanked Ellie for her hospitality and others glared at her on their way out.

Ellie and Russell headed to the basement to chat with that group of people, and Gramps and Gram lingered on the main floor. A huge weight had been lifted off Eva's shoulders.

They'd done their part to warn people. Now everything could go back to normal. Maybe everything would be okay now.

Something out the window grabbed Eva's attention. She watched the sky darken as if something big had suddenly gone in front of the setting sun. "Look," she said, as she hopped up from her seat and went to the window. Alex was right behind her. The hair on her arms stood up as she watched shadows crawl across the sky, pouring out their darkness, an evil storm. The shadows completed their path, erasing all the light from the world, and everything went dark.

Also by Jenni DeWitt

Eternal Light

Book 2 - Faith and Shadows Series

Why Won't God Talk to Me?

Surprising Ways He Already Is

Forty Days

A Memoir of Our Time in the Desert of Childhood Cancer

Find all Jenni's books at:

www.jennidewitt.com

~

Please review Visible and Invisible

on Amazon or Goodreads.

www.ingramcontent.com/pod-product-compliance
Lightning Source LLC
LaVergne TN
LVHW100522110826
845146LV00002B/742

* 9 7 9 8 9 9 1 7 1 3 3 1 3 *